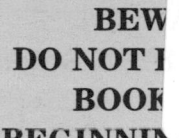

Cool! You've heard Madame Zapp's arcade has the most advanced virtual reality games ever made.

Want to try the Arctic Adventure? It seems so real you can't stop shivering. Can you keep warm long enough to track down the Abominable Snow Woman? Or check out "Adrift off Vega" and pick your alien foe: a two-headed Vegan, a giant cockroach, or a deadly yellow blob.

But be careful. There's something you don't know about these games. Something horrifying . . .

This scary adventure is all about you. You decide what will happen. And you decide how terrifying the scares will be!

Start on Page 1. Then follow the instructions at the bottom of each page. You make the choices. If you choose well, you'll return to the real world unharmed. But if you make the wrong choice . . . BEWARE!

SO TAKE A DEEP BREATH. CROSS YOUR FINGERS. AND TURN TO PAGE 1 TO *GIVE YOURSELF GOOSEBUMPS!*

READER BEWARE —
YOU CHOOSE THE SCARE!

Look for more
GIVE YOURSELF GOOSEBUMPS adventures
from R.L. STINE

#1 *Escape from the Carnival of Horrors*
#2 *Tick Tock, You're Dead!*
#3 *Trapped in Bat Wing Hall*
#4 *The Deadly Experiments of Dr. Eeek*
#5 *Night in Werewolf Woods*
#6 *Beware of the Purple Peanut Butter*
#7 *Under the Magician's Spell*
#8 *The Curse of the Creeping Coffin*
#9 *The Knight in Screaming Armor*
#10 *Diary of a Mad Mummy*
#11 *Deep in the Jungle of Doom*
#12 *Welcome to the Wicked Wax Museum*
#13 *Scream of the Evil Genie*
#14 *The Creepy Creations of Professor Shock*
#15 *Please Don't Feed the Vampire!*
#16 *Secret Agent Grandma*
#17 *Little Comic Shop of Horrors*
#18 *Attack of the Beastly Baby-sitter*
#19 *Escape from Camp Run-for-Your-Life*
#20 *Toy Terror: Batteries Included*
#21 *The Twisted Tale of Tiki Island*
#22 *Return to the Carnival of Horrors*

R.L. STINE

GIVE YOURSELF

Goosebumps®

ZAPPED IN SPACE

AN
APPLE
PAPERBACK

SCHOLASTIC INC.
New York Toronto London Auckland Sydney

A PARACHUTE PRESS BOOK

ISBN 0-590-39774-5

12 11 10 9 8 7 6 5 4 3 2 1   7 8 9/9 0 1 2/0

Printed in the U.S.A.   40

First Scholastic printing, November 1997

"This can't be the place!" your friend Katy cries.

"It's the right address," your other friend, Jordan, replies. He reads from the yellow flyer: "112 Front Street."

You stare at the shabby brick building in disbelief. The windows are broken. The front steps are crumbling.

There's no way this crummy place can be the new virtual reality arcade!

But then you notice a cracked and faded sign:

MADAME ZAPP'S VIRTUAL REALITY ARCADE

"This *is* it," you exclaim.

What a letdown! Ever since you and your friends first saw the flyers, you've wanted to visit the arcade. You bicycled all the way here from the other side of town.

But this building looks as if it's been empty for years.

You and your friends climb the crumbling steps. A heavy wooden door stands partway open. Inside, it looks dark and cold.

"Let's go," Katy says nervously. "This dump is probably crawling with rats."

"Don't be a wimp," Jordan scoffs. "Let's check it out."

Go ahead — push the door open and step inside on PAGE 2.

2

You step inside and find yourself in a circular, neon-lit room. Posters line the walls. In between the posters stand small plastic booths. Each booth contains four bucket seats in front of complicated control panels.

You wonder why they put a high-tech room in such a junky building. It's almost as if the owner didn't want to attract too much attention.

"Cool!" Katy exclaims.

"Check out these posters!" Jordan cries.

You examine the nearest poster. It shows a kid fighting with a dinosaur. Another poster pictures an old-fashioned Western shoot-out. In another one, kids are white-water rafting.

"Wow!" you blurt out. "I'm dying to play one of these games!"

"*How interesting . . .*" whispers a chilling voice.

You jump in surprise. The voice cuts into you like a frigid wind.

Find out who's speaking on PAGE 3.

You turn around — and stare. Facing you is a tall woman dressed in filmy gray robes. A gray veil covers her face. She wears a wide-brimmed gray hat and gray gloves.

What's with the cover-up? you wonder. She's dressed for winter in the middle of summer.

"I'm Madame Zapp," the woman announces in a whispery voice. "Welcome to my arcade. You're my very first customers!"

You reach into your pocket for a coin. "Where do I put my quarters?"

Madame Zapp holds up her hands. You notice they are huge — bigger than Shaquille O'Neal's. So are her feet.

"First-time customers are free," she whispers.

"All right!" Jordan shouts.

"Before you start, my little friends, you must put on helmets and special gloves and boots. They are connected to a computer. A computer program makes the adventure seem real. Very real." Madame Zapp laughs.

"Okay. I'm ready to roll," you declare.

"Wait!" Madame Zapp orders. "There's just one problem."

What is it? Find out on PAGE 4.

"Only two adventures are available right now," Madame Zapp says. "'Abominable Snow Woman' and 'Adrift off Vega.'"

The poster for "Abominable Snow Woman" shows kids in a snowy field, fighting a fierce-looking bluish-white creature. Overhead, violet and yellow northern lights glimmer. "Adrift off Vega" shows a spaceship in front of a large yellow planet.

"What's 'Adrift off Vega' like?" you ask.

"It's a space adventure," Madame Zapp replies. "It's still got a few bugs. Personally, I recommend 'Abominable Snow Woman.'"

"What's the plot?" you ask.

"I don't want to ruin any surprises," she whispers hoarsely. Her deep, rumbling laugh echoes off the walls.

You ask, "What if we want to quit the game?"

"To end the game at any time, reach up and remove your helmet," she replies. "But you won't want to end it."

This lady is ultra-creepy, you think. But the games look excellent.

Enter the virtual reality booth on PAGE 72.

You rush over and grab the picture out of Jordan's hands.

Katy peers over your shoulder. "Lizards!" she cries.

You gaze at the picture. It shows a lizard family — a mother, father, and baby. But you know they aren't really lizards. For one thing, this isn't Earth.

For another thing, you don't remember ever seeing a lizard with such long, sharp teeth!

"I think we'd better get out of here before they come home," you remark. Strolling to the open door, you step outside.

Hot red sun sears your skin. Screaming in pain, you leap back into the house. You glance at your arms.

You got a sunburn in about a second!

"Forget that," you tell your friends. "We'll have to find someplace to hide while we figure out what to do next."

"Uh — I think it's too late," Katy murmurs. "Turn around."

You turn around — and come face-to-face with the owner of the house!

Don't make any sudden moves. Just go to PAGE 46.

6

Everything goes dark. Then the Abominable Snow Woman's voice sounds in your helmet. "You wanted to go home," she says, and laughs. "This device will send you home. But not to the home you are expecting!"

Uh-oh. That sounds bad!

Before you can rip the helmet off, a siren sounds. Your whole body buzzes. For just one moment, you feel as if you're flying. Then, with a thump, you land on something soft. The buzzing stops. And you can see again.

The helmet is gone. You're lying in a bed in a strange room. The room obviously belongs to a kid. Model airplanes hang from the ceiling. Schoolbooks line a shelf above a bed. A computer sits on a desk.

"Andy!" someone calls. "Are you in there?"

You glance around. There's no sign of Andy.

"He's not here!" you call back.

The door opens. "What do you mean you're not here, Andy?" a kind-looking woman says. "Or have you changed your name?"

You stare at the woman. You've never seen her before.

Where is Andy? Where is the control center? What's going on?

Find out on PAGE 107.

"We'll try yellow," you declare.

You and your friends prepare to begin the Yellow level. Your Vegan pal hands you a tiny bottle. "Take this," it says. "It may come in handy during the game."

"Can you give us any hints about the Yellow level?" you ask.

"There's no more time to talk," the alien replies. "The Arcturans are close to winning. All I can do is wish you good luck."

"Thanks a bunch!" you grumble. Some help that is!

The electrode in your ear begins to tingle.

A moment later the alien throws the On switch for the game.

Start playing on PAGE 88.

8

You run heavily toward the light. Now you see that it comes from a small flying saucer. You don't even stop to think about how weird that is. You just wave your arms frantically.

"Help!" you shout. "S.O.S.!"

The saucer dips down. A long, furry purple arm reaches out and grabs your wrists — just as the first blob reaches your feet.

The blob quickly oozes up to your ankles — then your legs. Its gooey surface clings revoltingly to your skin. The blob tugs, sucking you down toward the heavy planet.

But the purple hand has a strong grip on your wrists. It pulls up — hard.

Your arms feel as if they're being yanked out of their sockets. Your legs feel as if they're being stretched like taffy.

The blob pulls down.

The hand pulls up.

You're being pulled in half!

See who wins on PAGE 111.

"I hear the lizard. It's coming!" Jordan cries.

"Quick!" you urge your friends. "Plaster the palm goo on yourselves!" You bend down and grab two handfuls of purple goo.

It's as thick as motor oil. It's so sticky, you can hardly spread it. It smells like garbage that's been left out too long.

You don't care. You spread the disgusting stuff all over your face, arms, and hands. Then you and your friends head for the door — just as the lizard enters the greenhouse.

HISSSSSS! It peers around, searching for you.

"This way, frog-face!" you call. "I dare you to come get us!"

Will your plan work? Find out on PAGE 43.

Your foot goes right to the floor.

The brakes don't work!

The snowmobile speeds straight toward the rock-hard glacier.

Frantically, you pull on the handlebars. Somehow, you've got to turn to the side, and quick!

But it's too late. You're going too fast.

Just before you become a kid-sicle, you think that maybe you should have let Andy win the arm-wrestling match. Maybe you shouldn't have tried so hard to get your own way. In fact, you resolve that in the future —

SPLAT!

"Let's head back," you whisper to Andy.

He nods. At the same instant, you both wheel around and start walking quickly back along the tunnel.

"ROWWWWF! ROWWWWF!"

Uh-oh! The Ice Hound is after you! You start to run.

You glance over your shoulder. The Ice Hound is gaining.

"Faster!" you shout to Andy. "Faster!"

Then you hear a dull roaring from behind you. When you glance over your shoulder again, you gasp.

The tunnel behind you is collapsing.

The pounding feet of the huge dog are causing a cave-in!

As you watch, a ton of ice and snow falls down between you and the Ice Hound. "NOOOOOO!" Andy screams as a wall of ice races toward you.

You and Andy are knocked off your feet. You cover your head with your arms. You're about to be buried alive!

But instead, the wall of ice pushes you and Andy forward. You skid along the tunnel and pop out the cave's entrance.

The next thing you know, you're rolling down the mountain.

To see where you land, turn to PAGE 50.

12

"The item that's not on the list is one human bone," you tell the Arcturans.

For a moment all three bald heads gaze at you. Then, at the same moment, they begin to laugh.

"That's wrong!" the blue-eyed head cackles. "I knew there was no way mere humans could beat our test!"

"Wait!" Jordan cries. "*I* know the right answer. Give us another chance!"

"No more chances!" the Arcturan replies. "To the spice mines with all of you!"

Blue energy sizzles toward you from the three heads. "Run!" you shout, and turn to flee from the room.

But before you've gone three steps, a tingling feeling sweeps over you. Ooooohhh, you feel so dizzy. . . .

The next thing you know, the whole world turns black.

Go on to PAGE 21.

When the larva has nearly reached you, you shout, "Now!"

The larva fills the tunnel. You squeeze between it and the walls. Its squishy body feels like a slimy water balloon.

"Climb up!" you urge your friends.

"It's totally yucky!" Katy complains.

"It's our only chance," you point out. Bracing yourself against the tunnel wall, you grab a fold of the larva's skin. It's like grabbing a handful of thick jelly.

Your hands and front are covered with slime. But you hang on and pull yourself up the creature's back. You offer a hand to Katy. She helps Jordan on.

The larva doesn't seem to notice that it has passengers. It begins to crawl straight up the side tunnel. You and your friends hug the monster's squishy body to keep from sliding off.

It's horrible!

Finally, you spot reddish daylight to your left. You and your friends slide off the larva's back. The light comes from a large hole in the tunnel wall. Through the hole, you see a set of stairs leading downward.

A sign above the stairs says: TO GARDEN OF DOOM.

Take the stairs to PAGE 68.

Jordan's and Katy's screams fill the lifeboat. The only reason you're not screaming too is because you're speechless with horror.

The creature that crawls through the hatch is . . . a roach.

A three-foot-tall cockroach!

Its slimy brown head is as big as a beach ball. Its six jointed legs are covered with stiff hairs. Its long, flexible antennas sweep through the air toward you.

With every step it takes, you hear a clicking noise.

As you watch, another roach squeezes in beside the first one. Then another squeezes through — and another — and another.

Dozens of giant roaches are crawling aboard the lifeboat.

Hurry over to PAGE 74.

The thing in the doorway is eight feet tall. Its smooth green skin is covered with grayish slime. Its has two heads with giant, lidless eyes. And it's got *four* long, ropy arms — each with wicked, clawed fingers.

"Ewwwww!" Katy cries. "Gross!"

"It's an alien!" Jordan exclaims. "I guess the game is starting. Maybe we're supposed to fight it."

The alien stomps toward you. Its feet leave puddles of slime, like a snail. You glance around for weapons. But all you see are some empty boxes. No verteron-ray guns or light swords.

The alien's four arms wave wildly. Black drops of goo fly from its fingers and land on Katy's skin.

"Ow!" she cries. "It burns!"

"Don't be dumb," Jordan scoffs. "How can it burn? This is virtual reality. You can't get hurt here!"

"That's what you think!" Katy snaps. She holds up her arm. Ugly red blisters are popping up all over her skin.

"Cool!" Jordan exclaims. "That looks totally real."

"It *is* real!" Katy complains. "This is no fun. I'm getting out of this game." She reaches up and pulls off her virtual reality helmet.

And then she screams.

What's going on? Find out on PAGE 115.

16

$$816$$
$$3\_7$$
$$492$$

"This is a magic square, made of the numbers one through nine," the green-eyed Arcturan tells you. "All the numbers across, down, and diagonally should add up to the same thing — fifteen. But the number in the center is missing." The Arcturan cackles. "Here's the challenge: What is the missing number?"

You gnaw on a fingernail. Math was never your best subject.

But you're better at it than Katy or Jordan.

It's up to you.

You gaze at the magic square. Then you whisper briefly to Katy and Jordan.

"Sounds good to me," Jordan declares. "Go for it."

Go ahead — take your best shot.

If you think the missing number is six, go to PAGE 128.

If you think it's five, turn to PAGE 102.

The blob oozes along the spongy ground.

Soon it's flowing over your sneaker. It slimes up your foot and begins to ooze toward your ankle. Its breathing grows louder.

"Yuck!" you cry. You try to kick it away.

But the blob won't let go of your foot.

Your heart pounds. "Get it off me!" you cry.

"Take off your shoe!" Katy orders.

Quickly, you kick your sneaker off. The blob goes with it. You can only stare in horror as your shoe disappears into the pulsing yellow mass.

A moment later the creature makes a burping noise.

Then it oozes out in three directions at once.

It's going after you, Jordan, and Katy!

"Let's get out of here," Katy urges. "Run, you guys!"

"Are you nuts?" Jordan retorts. "I'm bigger than you two. I'm so heavy, I can hardly move!"

"Wait!" you call. "The Vegan gave us a bottle. Maybe there's something in it that we can use to fight the blob."

You dig the bottle out of your pocket and hold it up.

Hey! It's empty!

If you run from the blob, turn to PAGE 24.
Battle it with the bottle on PAGE 22.

18

"We've forgotten something," you whisper to Andy. "We're in a computer program. Maybe we can make the program crash. That would definitely get rid of her."

Andy stares at you. "What about us?" he asks.

You shrug. "I don't know. We'll just have to see whether we make it back to reality or not."

"Okay," Andy says after a minute. "What do we do?"

"We have to put in more information than the computer's memory can handle," you explain. "I'll bet this program only handles English. Do you speak another language?"

"Only Pig Latin," Andy replies.

"Try it," you urge. "Just say anything."

"Okay. Rrrr-bay! I'm-way ery-vay old-cay," Andy begins.

"Ee-may oo-tay," you agree. "Is-thay etter-bay ork-way ast-fay."

The Abominable Snow Woman stares suspiciously at you. "What are you doing?" she demands. She thrusts out her hands, and blue sparks shoot from her fingertips. "You will never —"

Then, all of a sudden, she freezes — in the middle of her sentence. Her hideous mouth hangs open.

Quick, before you *freeze, turn to PAGE 25.*

"But how — how —" you sputter.

"Here's the deal," Andy explains. "Somehow, the game booth transformed us into electronic images. We only exist inside the game. Whatever happens in here really happens to us."

You try not to freak out — but you fail.

"We've got to get out of here!" you shout.

"The only escape is by finding and defeating the Abominable Snow Woman," Andy tells you. "That's how the game works."

Before you can ask any questions, a thunderous roar fills the air. Something large and white comes bounding toward you.

"It looks like a polar bear!" Andy cries.

Whatever it is — you now know it can hurt you. Your mouth is dry. Your legs are quivering.

Then you hear an even louder sound. *CRAAAAACK!*

You spin around. A small iceberg has broken off from the snowfield. It bobs out to the gray Arctic sea.

When you turn again, the white beast is closer to you. You still can't see what it is. But it's way big.

To stay and face the beast, turn to PAGE 93.

To escape on the floating iceberg, go to PAGE 91.

20

"Make snowballs to throw at the bird!" you scream at Andy. "Pack them hard, so they sting."

You and Andy furiously build an arsenal of snowballs. As the bird approaches, you cock your arms, ready to throw.

It's getting closer and closer ... just another second.

At last the pelican is within striking distance. "Fire!" you shout.

Snowballs fly at the pelican.

Did it work? Find out on PAGE 83.

You wake up in darkness. A delicious smell of cinnamon fills your nostrils. It smells like someone is baking apple pie.

"Mmmmm," Katy murmurs. "I smell vanilla."

"No —" Jordan interrupts. "It's chocolate. Pure chocolate!"

As your eyes adjust to the dim light, you gaze around. You seem to be in a large, rocky cavern. Strangely enough, you can't spot any stoves or kitchen equipment. But you can make out dim shapes moving by the walls.

"I'm hungry!" Jordan shouts.

"Me too!" Katy cries.

"Me three," you agree.

The scents are driving you crazy. Your mouth waters uncontrollably. You've never been so hungry in your life.

But where are the delicious smells coming from?

Then you hear footsteps.

Yes! Maybe someone has come to feed you!

Turn to PAGE 42.

22

You stare at the little bottle in dismay. The Vegan said it might help you.

But how do you fight a giant blob with an empty bottle?

The blob oozes toward you. *SHHH, SHHH,* goes its breathing.

"Maybe it's some sort of secret weapon," you say hopefully. You prepare to throw the bottle at the blob.

"Wait!" Katy calls. "Maybe you're supposed to put the blob *in* the bottle."

Maybe she's right. It doesn't look possible, but —

"Yeah, right," Jordan sneers. "That's like trying to put a car inside a shoe box! Throw the bottle."

Hmm. Jordan has a point too.

To try to put the blob in the bottle, turn to PAGE 31.

Throw the bottle at the blob on PAGE 45.

You know the answer to that question. "The bats' claws weren't on the list," you declare confidently.

For a moment, all three heads just stare at you.

"I don't believe it!" the blue-eyed Arcturan cries at last.

"What? You're not saying I'm wrong, are you?" you ask.

"No!" the creature snaps. "You're right. *That's* what I don't believe. How could someone with a head as puny as yours be right about anything?" Its mouth turns down in a frown.

"Our heads are just the right size!" Katy cries indignantly.

"Yeah. And we're ready for the next challenge," you add.

The Arcturan smiles nastily. "The next challenge is a difficult math problem. I'm sure you Earthlings can't possibly figure it out."

"We just might surprise you," Jordan boasts.

The Arcturan rolls its blue eyes. "I doubt it."

The wall behind the three Arcturan heads lights up. In blue writing, the challenge appears.

Give it a try on PAGE 16.

"Let's get out of here!" you cry.

"You got it!" Katy agrees. "Run!"

You turn and try to run from the blob. But you can only move in slow motion. Your legs feel as heavy as an elephant's legs. Every step feels as if you're climbing a steep mountain with a hundred-pound pack. The most you can manage is a slow walk.

"Faster!" Katy urges.

"I'm moving as fast as I can!" Jordan snaps.

You glance back. The blob is slow too.

But it's gaining on you. *SHHH, SHHHH*, it breathes.

"Keep going!" you yell. "We have to outrun it!"

"I can't!" Jordan whines. He's moving even more slowly. And then — he trips and falls. The blob flows over his legs.

"Help!" Jordan wails. "It's got me!"

Ooze over to PAGE 113.

Everything is frozen. You can't move or speak. Neither can Andy. Even the sparks from the Abominable Snow Woman's fingers hang motionless in midair.

Then, after a few seconds, you're able to move again.

"It's working. The computer froze!" you shout to Andy. "It can't handle Pig Latin! Eep-kay alking-tay!"

"I'm running out of things to say," he gasps. "I mean, I'm-way unning-ray out-way of-way ingsthay o-tay ay-say."

"Ing-say!" you suggest. "Ell-tay a-way okejay!"

Suddenly, ghostly words and symbols start to appear in the air. A message from the computer's hard drive! It reads: MEMORY SHORTAGE — CLOSE LANGUAGE FILES IMMEDIATELY.

The Snow Woman stomps toward you. But you keep up your torrent of nonsense words. The computer sends out another warning message: SYSTEM OVERLOAD! SYSTEM OVERLOAD!

The Snow Woman's hand clamps over your mouth. You can't speak.

But Andy can! Just as he yells, "Is-thay amegay inks-stay!" the world goes totally black. Except for one shrinking white dot — right where the Abominable Snow Woman was standing.

Finally, the dot vanishes with a *POP*!

Return to the real world on PAGE 84.

26

You find yourself in a narrow, icy tunnel. In the dim light, you see Andy and the Ice Hound up ahead. You hurry to catch up.

The dog speeds up. The tunnel grows darker. You scramble forward.

"Where's he taking us?" you wonder aloud.

"Maybe the Abominable Snow Woman lives deep in the cave," Andy replies.

You keep following the dog. But after several minutes, you still haven't gotten to the end. And the tunnel is almost pitch-black now.

"I'm going back," you tell Andy. "We're not getting anywhere."

"I guess you're right," he agrees.

The two of you turn around and start back to the main cave.

You've taken two steps when you hear a terrifying growl.

Turn to PAGE 61.

A blinding light forces your eyes shut. You feel as if you're on an elevator that's plunging down out of control.

The falling feeling suddenly stops. You open your eyes.

You're in a rose-colored room with red tile floors. Red and pink couches, chairs, and tables are scattered about. The warm air smells faintly of flowers. All is still and silent.

"We're in someone's living room," Katy whispers.

She's right. One wall of the room is covered with framed pictures. Crossed swords hang on another wall. Next to them is a rifle. Instead of a trigger, it has a collection of dials and knobs. It must be an energy weapon, you think.

Through the large windows, you see bare, scorching desert. A clear pink sky arches over hot red sand. Strange, scraggly weeds poke up through the sand. A red sun blazes overhead.

"Whoa!" Katy exclaims. "I wonder who lives here?"

"There's a picture of them over here," Jordan replies, pulling a framed photo off the wall. His face goes pale. "Uh-oh," he mutters. "I think we're in trouble."

Turn to PAGE 5.

28

This one is a no-brainer.

"Quick!" you cry. "Let's get out before the alien returns!" You yank a lever underneath the hatch. It springs open. You and your friends crawl through.

The hatch clangs shut. You glance around.

You're in a small room with four swivel chairs and a control panel in the wall. A sign on the control panel says EMERGENCY LIFEBOAT. PRESS RED BUTTON TO START.

You press the red button. A horn goes *AOOOOGAH! AOOOOGAH!*

"Oh, no!" Katy cries. "They'll hear us!"

But the lifeboat starts up with a thump. You feel it begin to drift. You hear a loud whooshing noise, and the small ship takes off. You glance through the porthole.

"We did it!" you exclaim. "We got away!"

Your small craft is pulling away from the huge alien ship. From here, the alien ship looks like a big blimp.

The lifeboat moves farther and farther from the alien craft. Soon the big ship is just a speck in the distance.

You're adrift in space!

Drift to PAGE 105.

Katy and Jordan take off through an open doorway. Their footsteps pound down the hall.

Quickly, you grab a sword from the wall. Holding the weapon in front of you, you face your attacker.

The lizard's red tongue darts out of its mouth. Now you notice that its fingers end in long, sharp, curved claws.

One swipe of those claws could rip you to pieces!

You grip the sword tighter.

The lizard jumps at you, hissing.

In terror, you swing the sword. *WHAP!*

You don't mean to, but your wild swing chops off the lizard's hand! The scaly creature screams. Green blood spurts all over the red tile.

Gross! You concentrate on holding the sword ready — and not hurling.

The lizard hisses and grabs at you with its other hand.

THOCK! You slice that one off too.

The lizard's beady eyes fill with pain and rage.

You lower the sword. "Get lost before I make you into a wallet!" you taunt.

But you forgot one thing.

What is it? Turn to PAGE 49.

30

"We're going to crash!" you scream as the alien ship fills the porthole. You close your eyes. You can't watch.

"Wait!" Katy shouts. "What's that?"

You open your eyes. A bright beam of blue light shoots out from the alien spacecraft. It encircles your little ship.

The lifeboat slows down.

It stops spinning.

A big cargo bay slides open in the alien spacecraft.

The lifeboat moves toward the opening.

"It's a tractor beam!" Jordan cries. "We're saved!"

"What do you mean, we're saved?" you snap. You punch frantically at the controls. But you can't get free of the blue beam. "We're right back where we started. And now we have to fight the alien!"

Crawl back through the hatch to PAGE 48.

"I'm going to try Katy's idea," you announce. You lean down, holding the bottle out toward the blob.

To your surprise, the blob starts to flow *into* the bottle.

"No way!" Jordan gasps in surprise.

"I told you!" Katy exclaims.

You can't believe your eyes. But the blob continues to flow inside the bottle. How can something so big fit into such a tiny container?

In a few moments, the entire blob is inside the bottle.

"It worked!" Katy cries. "We won!"

Jordan snorts. "If we won, how come we're still on this planet? The Vegan said we'd return to the game center."

"Yeah," you agree. You gaze at the bottle and think.

You've captured the alien blob. But there must be something more to the game. Something else you're supposed to do.

"Let me see it," Katy asks. She takes the bottle and peers in. "It smells like lemon custard," she announces.

"Hey!" You snap your fingers. "Maybe that's the answer!"

Turn to PAGE 39.

"I'll go first," you volunteer bravely. You take a deep breath and dip a finger into the bottle.

It comes out covered with slimy yellow goo.

Do you really dare taste it?

Your hand shakes as you lick your finger.

For just a moment, you feel like throwing up. Then you swallow. "Hey, it's sort of . . . good!" you tell your friends. "It really does taste like lemon custard!"

You pour a little of the goo into Katy's palm. Her doubtful expression vanishes after her first taste. "Yum!" she cries.

You and your friends pass the bottle around. In only a few moments it's empty. You run your finger around the rim and lick off the last sweet drops.

WHISSSSSSSH! A strong wind begins to blow. It sweeps the greenish-yellow mist away. When the wind dies down, you find yourselves back in the Vegan game room.

If you haven't yet completed the Red level, go to PAGE 95.

If you have completed the Red level, begin the Blue level on PAGE 104.

You and your friends grab more cartons and throw them as fast as you can. One of the cartons lands over one of the creature's heads. Another carton covers the other head.

The alien lets out a high-pitched squeak of pain and confusion. It begins to stagger in circles.

"It can't see!" Katy cries.

The alien squeaks in panic. It falls heavily to the floor. Its arms wave feebly in the air.

You approach the alien, holding another carton. You kick a carton off one of the creature's heads. Then you kick off the second carton.

"No!" the alien squeaks. "Don't hit me again!"

"What a wimp!" Jordan mutters.

"I won't hit you — if you promise to return us to Earth," you announce in your deepest voice.

The alien gazes meekly up at you. Tears flow out of its eyes.

"I'm sorry," it says. "That is impossible."

Why? Turn to PAGE 92.

34

You're certain that the colors were violet and yellow. "Let's take the left-hand door," you tell Andy.

He shrugs. "Okay."

The door opens onto a long hall. At the far end is another door with a sign saying OFFICE.

You approach the door and knock. A voice calls, "Come in."

Inside, you stop and stare in surpise. The person waiting for you is a tall woman dressed in gray robes and a gray veil.

"Madame Zapp!" you cry. "What are *you* doing here?"

"I live here," she answers. "This is my domain."

Huh? Okay. She's weird. But you can't worry about that now. "Well, I'm glad we ran into you," you hurry on. "We're looking for the Abominable Snow Woman. We want to exit this game."

Madame Zapp laughs. "No one leaves this game unless the Abominable Snow Woman agrees," she tells you. "And she won't."

"How do you know?" Andy demands.

"Haven't you guessed?" Madame Zapp murmurs.

Then she pulls off her veil.

You scream in terror.

If you have the nerve, go on to PAGE 124.

You're in a large room. The metal walls are painted gray. On your left is a heavy, round door. On your right, a huge window through which you see millions of stars. Beneath the window, you notice a small hatchway.

It's perfect! Just the way you imagined a spaceship would look.

You peer out the window. A big reddish planet with yellow rings swims into view. It looks kind of like Saturn — but the colors are different.

"This is a way cool ship!" Jordan exclaims.

"Yeah. And it really looks like there's a planet out there," Katy comments, gazing into the blackness.

You reach out to touch the thick Plexiglas of the window. It's cold. You knock on a metal wall. *CLANG!*

"It all seems so real," you agree. "It's awesome! I wonder when the adventure starts?"

At that moment the big, round door crashes open.

Even though you know the game isn't real, you can't help screaming when you see what fills the doorway.

Scream on over to PAGE 15.

"I win!" Andy shouts, jumping around. "I'm number one! I'm number one!"

"Relax," you grumble. "You didn't win the lottery."

"I always wanted to drive a snowmobile," Andy admits. "This is my big chance. As soon as I beat the Abominable Snow Woman, I'll get you out of here."

He climbs onto the snowmobile and switches on the ignition.

Nothing happens.

"Put your foot on the gas," you advise.

Andy switches the key again. He steps on the gas.

VROOM! VROOM! VROOOM!

But the snowmobile doesn't move.

"Let me try," you offer. Pushing him aside, you climb into the seat and rev the engine.

VROOOM! KAPLOOOOOOOOP!

Smoke fills the air.

"Jump!" Andy shouts. "It's on fire!"

Jump to PAGE 82.

In terror, you shake the blob off your body. "Let's get out of here!" you shout to Katy.

"Help me!" Katy screams.

Oh, no. The blob is covering her arms! It spreads to her chest. You grab her legs and try to pull her away.

But it's too late. In seconds, she's a blob too. Your two best friends have turned into mounds of lemon Jell-O.

And they're both oozing toward you!

You turn to run.

But you can't run on this heavy planet.

You move as fast as you can. The blobs ooze after you. Shaking in terror, you put one heavy leg after another. You've got to get away!

But where can you go? You're all alone on an alien planet. Earth is thousands of light-years away.

There's no hope. No hope at all.

You think about giving up and becoming a blob.

No way! You're not ready for that yet.

Especially when you see a light moving toward you.

Run to the light on PAGE 8.

38

The lead roach reaches for you.

You grab the fire extinguisher. You aim it at the big bug. "Back off, bug!" you scream, and press the handle.

Cold, wet foam sprays out the end of the extinguisher.

The cockroach makes a high-pitched screaming noise. It scrambles out of the way. Foam splashes some of the other roaches. They all panic, crawling up the walls and skittering across the ceiling.

You keep spraying the fire extinguisher. Katy and Jordan cheer you on. Roaches scuttle everywhere in panic. Several of the giant insects bump the lifeboat's controls. The small ship lurches and bounces like a toy boat in a flood.

Finally all the roaches squeeze through the hatch to their own ship. Quickly, you slam the hatch shut.

But the lifeboat is spinning out of control.

Turn to PAGE 109.

Katy stares at you. "Maybe *what* is the answer?"

"Look. Somehow, we have to get rid of this blob, right?" you say to your friends. "I mean, how else can we get back to the Vegans? Now, the blob *looks* like food. It *smells* like food."

"Hold on!" Jordan makes a face. "If you're going to say what I think you're going to say — don't."

"What are you going to say?" Katy wants to know.

"It's the only thing that makes sense," you argue.

"WILL YOU PLEASE TELL ME WHAT YOU'RE TALKING ABOUT?" Katy shouts. Her face is red. "*What* makes sense? How can we win?"

You take a deep breath. "We have to eat the blob."

"Eww! Gross!" Katy cries. "I wish you hadn't told me that. I think I'm going to barf."

"It makes me want to hurl too," you admit. "But it might be our only way out of here!"

Eat the blob on PAGE 32.

40

"It's an insect nursery!" you exclaim. "These round things are eggs."

"No way!" Jordan cries.

Then the tunnel fills with a long, squishy, rounded blob. It must be twelve feet long. It's gray and eyeless. But it does have a mouth. A big, round mouth lined with tiny, pointed teeth.

Katy gasps. "What is that?"

"It's a larva — a baby insect," you whisper. You recently studied ants in science class. And you remember your teacher saying that the baby ants are *always* hungry.

Uh-oh.

The blind larva squelches along the tunnel toward you. Its huge mouth opens and closes, opens and closes. It's an eating machine — and once it reaches you, there will be no way to avoid those terrifying, sharp teeth.

Maybe, if you crawl into one of the egg holes, the hideous larva will pass you right by.

Or maybe you should try to outrun the creature.

To run down the tunnel, turn to PAGE 101.

To crawl into one of the egg holes and hide, go to PAGE 64.

In an instant, the beam of focused light melts a chunk from the center of the pillar! The pillar collapses.

Now the floor begins to shake. A thundering noise fills the cave. Sharp bits of ice break off and plunge from the ceiling.

With a deafening *WHOOSH!* the cave collapses, burying you and Andy under a ton of white powder.

Snow long, sucker! And remember: Next time the sign says TAKE ONE — TAKE *ONE*!

THE END

42

A fat, short, three-headed creature appears. Its skin is covered with jagged spikes. It looks like a walking rock.

"Why aren't you three working?" the creature demands.

Before you can answer, the creature shoves a pick into your hands. "Get going — the spices are ripe!" it bellows.

At last you can see well enough to make out the movement by the walls. It's other creatures. Dozens of them — in every size and shape. They're digging at the walls with picks and shovels!

"What is going on?" you ask the three-headed creature. "Where are we?"

"Where do you think?" it snarls. "The spice mines." It hands you a pick and swats you. "Now get moving!"

You swing your pick at the walls of the mine. With each crack of the pick, another delicious smell fills your nose. But, somehow, you're not so hungry anymore.

Too bad — but this spicy adventure has come to a tasteless

END!

"Come on, fly-breath!" you cry to the alien. "Let's go play outside!"

The lizard doesn't understand English. But it gets your drift. It leaps toward you. You move closer to the exit.

"Bet you can't eat just one human!" you goad the lizard.

It roars in anger. You move even closer to the exit.

Just as the lizard jumps at you, Jordan throws the door open.

The three of you rush outside. Hot desert air fills your lungs. But your skin is completely protected by the purple goo.

The lizard leaps onto the desert sand — and screams. Ten seconds later, it bursts into flames.

Thirty seconds after that, it's just a heap of ashes.

A flash of red light fills the desert air. When it dies away, you find yourselves back in the Vegan battle room.

"Congratulations!" your alien captor booms. "You won the Red level!"

If you've already won the Yellow level, go on to the Blue level on PAGE 104.

Otherwise, you'll want to move on to the Yellow level on PAGE 7.

44

You cross through the blue doorway into a large white room. Blue-tinted sunlight streams in from a high window.

At one end of the room stand three small tables. On top of each table is a round glass case, like an upside-down fishbowl.

Inside each case is a big bald head!

"Whoa," Jordan murmurs.

"Gross," Katy declares.

You stare at the heads. They look human, but their skin is pale blue. Their eyes are open. But they don't move or blink.

Are they alive?

"Welcome to Arcturus," the head with blue eyes pipes.

You jump. Then, summoning your nerve, you approach the heads. "Wh-where are your bodies?" you ask.

"We Arcturans have outgrown the need for bodies. We spend all our time thinking," the green-eyed head replies. "It gives you a superior smile."

And then the third, brown-eyed Arcturan asks you a question that totally surprises you.

Read the question on PAGE 112.

"I'm going to throw the bottle," you decide. "Maybe it's filled with invisible gas or something."

You toss the bottle into the center of the pulsating mass.

The blob surrounds the bottle. After a second there's a muffled thud. The yellow mass heaves and bubbles.

"It worked!" Jordan cries. "You killed it!"

"Yes!" Katy exclaims. "What an awesome shot! You are —"

"Quiet," you interrupt. You're trying to hear whether the blob is still breathing. But your friends are talking too much — blah, blah, blah. You can't hear a thing.

The blob heaves again. Suddenly the bottle shoots out like a rocket. *WHAM!* It whacks you in the head.

"OOOOHHH," you moan, sliding to the spongy ground.

That's the last thing you remember — until you wake up feeling wonderful. The heaviness is gone. You sniff in a deep breath of greenish-yellow mist. Mmm, does it smell good!

You stretch your slimy yellow body happily. Oh, well, you think. So you became a blob after all. It's not so bad. You don't have to eat. Or sleep. Or even talk to your friends. No more blah, blah, blah.

From now on it's just blob, blob, blob!

THE END

46

Well, you aren't quite face-to-face. The lizard-creature hasn't seen you yet. It's busy taking off a long coat made of shiny silver material.

You stand frozen, staring at the alien. It's covered with red scales. A long red tongue flicks out between its sharp teeth.

It hangs the coat on a hook, then turns around. Its small, evil black eyes land on you.

Instantly, the scales on its back rise up. They make a buzzing sound, like a rattlesnake. It opens its mouth and hisses.

Then it leaps toward you.

"It's attacking!" Jordan screams.

Desperately, you glance around the room. The weapons on the wall catch your eye.

"Run!" you call to your friends. "I'll hold it off!"

Which should you try? A sword? Or the energy weapon?

Decide fast!

Take a sword on PAGE 29.
Try the energy weapon on PAGE 110.

You and Andy enter the hallway. Its icy walls sparkle like diamonds. It's almost blinding. Already, you feel confused — and you haven't even gone anywhere yet.

You want to head north. But you have no idea which way north is. The hall branches off to the right and left. The branches branch.

In no time, you are majorly mixed up.

"Where are we?" Andy cries.

"How should I know?" you retort. "Just keep walking!"

Then you turn a corner — and find yourself in a roomful of circuits and switches. A virtual reality booth is attached to one wall. Two helmets are wired into the booth. There's a red switch on the wall above the helmets. By the switch hangs a sign: HOMING DEVICE.

"This must be the control room!" Andy cries. "We did it! Come on. Let's put on the helmets!"

"Wait!" you object. "This is too easy. Why isn't the Abominable Snow Woman stopping us?"

"Who knows?" Andy responds. "Who cares? All I know is, this looks like the way out!"

Maybe Andy's right. Maybe you did find the way out.

You place the helmet on your head and pull the red switch.

Go on to PAGE 6.

"Okay, listen up. We have to work together if we're going to beat this slimy alien," you say quickly.

The only possible weapons in the hold are the empty cartons. They're not much — but they're better than nothing. Each of you picks up a carton.

And then you wait.

A moment later, the door opens. The alien slithers in.

"*Now!*" you shout. You hurl your box at the hideous creature.

"*EEEEYAAAAH!*" Katy shouts, throwing her carton.

"Take that, black-hole-breath!" Jordan yells, swinging a box like a club.

The alien throws its four arms in front of its faces to protect itself. One of the cartons slams into its stomach.

The alien screams in rage and bounds toward you and your friends. Hot globs of black goo from its fingers spray all over the room.

You scream as the acid goop splatters you. "Keep throwing stuff!" you shout to your friends. "It's our only hope!"

Go to PAGE 33.

Even on Earth, some injured lizards can grow new tails.

Here they can grow new arms! In front of your eyes, the lizard's hands begin to grow back.

The new claws look even sharper than the old ones.

As you stare, the lizard pounces. It pins you to the floor. Its hot, stinking breath blasts in your face.

In a desperate move, you slash at its neck.

SNICK! The sharp sword slices off the lizard's head.

The head rolls to the floor, blood oozing from its neck.

But the lizard doesn't let go of you! It continues to hold you down — while a new head starts to grow.

In horror, you watch as a tiny bump grows from the lizard's neck. The bump grows bigger. A pair of tiny black eyes appear. Then a tiny mouth.

The mouth opens, revealing dozens of dagger-like teeth.

It looks as if you're the one who's going to be a wallet!

You hope Jordan and Katy managed to get away. Maybe, you think, they'll find a way to defeat the creature someday. But unfortunately, this time the lizard came out a*head.*

THE END

50

WUMMPPPFFF!

You and Andy land on a cold, wet, slushy surface.

Stunned, you lie there for a moment. Then you slowly pick yourself up. "I can't believe we're still alive!" you exclaim.

You check out the landscape. There's no sign of the cave entrance. Or of the Abominable Ice Hound. All you see is white, white snow in all directions. The Arctic sun is a pale disk in the distance.

"What happened? Where are we?" Andy wails.

"I'm not sure," you reply. "But don't panic."

"Don't panic? We're stuck in the middle of the Arctic!"

"Would you chill out?" you snap.

"Chill?" Andy grumbles. "I'm already frozen."

Then you spot a trail of footprints leading into the distance. The footprints look human, except for one thing: They're as big as tennis rackets.

"Look!" you cry, pointing.

Andy inspects them. "I bet they were made by the Abominable Snow Woman," he declares. "She's supposed to be a giant!"

Follow the footprints to PAGE 99.

Blue skin and bits of blue brain fly in every direction. You cover your head with your arms.

"Oh, that is so gross!" Jordan gasps.

"I am definitely going to be sick now!" Gagging, Katy wipes exploded Arcturan off her arm.

A shimmering blue door appears in the middle of the room. The three of you stumble through it — and find yourselves back in the Vegan game room.

"Congratulations!" a familiar metallic voice cries. It's your Vegan friend. "We knew you could do it!" The Vegan shakes hands with all three of you at once.

"What happened to the Arcturans?" you ask.

"They couldn't believe someone beat them," the Vegan explains. "They exploded from an overload of anger."

"We did what you asked," you point out. "Now take us home."

"I'm sorry," the Vegan says. "We can't do that now."

Oh, no! What now? Find out on PAGE 114.

If you run the maze correctly, you'll beat the Abominable Snow Woman.

Using a pencil, trace a path from START to one of the numbers inside the maze. When you reach a number, turn to that page to see if you have won.

You and your friends strap yourself into your seats in the transporter. A thundering rumbling fills your ears. You're slammed back against your seat.

After several minutes, the pressure dies down. You open your eyes.

You're back at Madame Zapp's arcade!

"*WHEW!*" Jordan cries, unstrapping himself. "That was some adventure!"

"I'm glad to be back," you declare.

"Me too," Katy agrees. "It seemed so real!"

"It *was* real!" you protest.

But then you wonder — was it? Virtual reality is supposed to feel exactly like real life.

Did you just imagine that it was all really happening?

"Where's Madame Zapp?" Jordan asks.

You glance around. There's no sign of her. And then you notice something on the wall of the booth.

Something very gross.

Take a closer look on PAGE 60.

54

As soon as you complete the maze, you hear a shriek.

"No!" screams the Abominable Snow Woman. "Impossible! I won't let you win!"

"Ignore her!" Andy warns. "We have to reach the control center!"

You see the controls up ahead. A switch sits in the middle of the console.

Somehow, you have to get past the Snow Woman.

"Never!" she repeats. "You'll never get past me!" Her eyes begin to flash. Long blue sparks shoot out of her fingertips.

SNAP! CRACK! SPITZZZ!

While you watch in horror, she begins to grow. She becomes taller. She spreads out to the sides. Right before your eyes, she expands until she completely fills the space ahead of you.

There's no way you can get past her. No way you can get to the control center.

Unless . . .

You have a sudden, desperate idea.

Carry it out on PAGE 18.

You place your hands firmly around your neck, where the base of the helmet should be. You pull up.

Congratulations — all you managed to do was choke yourself!

You try again. You close your eyes. You concentrate.

You pull off the hood to your parka.

You open your eyes.

You're still in the Arctic. And your ears are freezing! Quickly, you tug the hood back on.

"I told you," Andy murmurs.

"This is a joke, right?" you demand, voice shaking. You yank off your gloves.

The result? Your hands start turning blue.

"No!" you cry. "I don't believe it!" Your heart begins to pound harder. Despite the cold, you're starting to sweat. You fight panic. This can't be happening!

But it *is* happening.

The virtual reality game is real. And you're stuck in it.

What next? Turn to PAGE 19.

You expect to see ice and snow.

Instead, you see a familiar-looking plastic booth.

You're back in the virtual reality arcade!

Melting the switch released you!

You've never been so happy to finish a game. You pull off your helmet and gaze around. Madame Zapp opens the booth door.

Jordan and Katy stand impatiently outside.

"We've been waiting forever," Jordan says. "Let's go home!"

"But —" You glance around, puzzled. "Where is Andy?"

"The other boy already left," Madame Zapp tells you.

"But what about the Abominable Snow Woman?" you ask. "We were trapped in the game! We couldn't get out!"

"I told you it would seem very real," Madame Zapp says. "Run along now, I'm closing up. Have an ice — uh, I mean nice — day." She shoves you quickly out the door.

You can't believe it! You were so sure everything that happened was real. You can't believe it's all over.

On the way home, you discover that it *isn't* over.

Not quite yet.

Huh? Turn to PAGE 69.

"Break the switch!" you instruct Andy.

He takes the shovel, raises it, and smashes it down on the switch.

KLANNNNNNNG! The vibrations rattle the fillings in your teeth. Again, Andy smashes the shovel on the switch.

KARPLOOK! KABLAMMMMMMINGGGGG! KAPLOOOOIE!

The switch snaps right off the machine. The machine bursts open. Gears, levers, sprockets, and wires fly out. Thick, gray, bitter-smelling steam hisses from the broken engine.

The nasty steam fills the air. You begin to choke. You try to open the door to escape. But the doorknob won't turn.

Uh-oh. If you don't get out soon, you'll smother!

You sink to the floor, gasping. Then you hear the door slam.

"Someone's here!" Andy cries. "We're saved!"

You glance up as a shadow looms through the thick steam.

And feel your heart sink to your toenails.

Why? Find out on PAGE 122.

You and Andy step to the back of the igloo. There you find several cartons full of frozen food.

You examine the rations. There are hundreds of labeled packages. They all seem to contain the same thing: rolls of rubbery dried fat.

"'Blubberburger,'" you read aloud. "'Blubber pudding, Swedish blubberballs.'"

"'Fried blubber on a stick,'" Andy reads. "'Blubberwurst.'" He makes a barfing sound. "It's all blubber. Gross!"

You bend down and read a sign pinned to one of the boxes. "This gives the date for the Abominable Snow Woman's next trip here," you announce.

Andy studies the sign. "Oh, no!" he cries. "That's nearly a year from now."

You and Andy stare at each other.

It seems neither of you will have much to do for the next year — except sit around and chew the fat.

THE END

Six roach soldiers hustle you, Jordan, and Katy off the spaceship. They march you to a door with a red light over it.

"Wh-what are you going to do with us?" Jordan stammers.

The roach soldiers just shove you through the door — into a room that looks and smells like a dump!

"Here you are. Excellent!" A truly enormous roach scurries toward you, ticking off items on a clipboard. "Take a seat. We'll start taping the program in a minute."

"Taping?" you repeat, totally confused.

"Yes, we're making a cooking show." The huge bug beams. "It's called *Garbage Magic*. Today the chef will make stir-fried coffee grounds and moldy lettuce pie. It's our very first TV program. You three humans are our TV experts."

"Gross — I mean, great," Katy murmurs with a sickly smile.

What can you do? You're trapped light-years from home on a world ruled by giant roaches. If they want you to help them make insect TV, you have to obey them. No matter how gross it is.

Well, Madame Zapp warned you there were bugs in the program. Guess she wasn't kidding!

THE END

60

You examine the substance closely. It's blue and green.

"It looks like — *EEEEEEWWWWW!*" Katy groans.

"It looks like an exploded Arcturan brain!" Jordan exclaims.

"That's what it is," says a familiar, hollow voice.

You jump and glance at the console. The Vegan's voice is coming through the speakers.

"What happened to Madame Zapp?" you demand.

"She worked for us. We planted her here to help us find smart Earth kids," the Vegan tells you. "But it seems she was really an Arcturan spy looking for game-playing tips. When you won the three challenges, her brain exploded."

"Yuck!" you mutter.

"Thank you all," the Vegan calls. There's a *CLICK* — and then its voice is gone for good.

But that's not the last you see of your alien friend. When you, Katy, and Jordan leave the arcade, you happen to glance up at the sky. Then you stop and stare. "Look!" you call, pointing.

Over your heads, a strange, blimplike ship is finishing a skywriting message. This is what it says:

GAME OVER — YOU WIN!

"GGGGRRRRRR!"

Your heart nearly stops in fright. The growling is coming from the friendly Ice Hound!

Suddenly it doesn't seem so friendly. It stands glaring at you. Its teeth are bared. Its white fur stands on end.

"Easy, pooch, easy," you plead.

"I don't think it wants us to turn back," Andy whispers.

You take a step back. The hound growls louder. It paces toward you.

You notice saliva dripping from its razor-sharp teeth. You remember how fast it can run. You recall how much you hate pain.

"I think we'd better keep following," Andy says.

You glance around in desperation. There's no escape, except back the way you came. What will you do?

Turn back on PAGE 11.
Follow the Ice Hound on PAGE 89.

62

You burst out laughing. "That's nuts!" you exclaim. "This isn't real. In real life, I'm sitting in Madame Zapp's virtual reality booth. You must be in the booth next to me."

Andy doesn't look like he's kidding. He says, "Days ago, I went to the virtual reality arcade and signed up for 'Abominable Snow Woman.' The next thing I knew, I was stuck inside the game. Since then, I've been trying to get out."

"Yeah, right." You snicker. How dumb does he think you are?

"Look at this," Andy retorts. He rolls up his sleeve. He shows you a thick, ugly scab on his arm. "I hurt myself my first day here. You think that could happen in a game?"

You remember the rip in your parka, and the cut you got.

But they weren't *real*, were they?

"I can prove this is all a computer game," you say. "I can end it any time just by taking off my helmet."

You reach up to remove the helmet.

Start pulling on PAGE 55.

"We found an odd number of words," you tell the aliens.

The first Arcturan glares at you. Its blue eyes bulge.

Suddenly you notice that its head is starting to swell! It seems to press against the sides of its glass case.

You glance at the other heads. They're bulging too.

"What's happening?" Katy whispers.

"I don't —" you start to say. But your words are cut off by the sound of shattering glass. The heads have grown right out of their cases!

Then —

SPLAT! SPLAT! SPLAT!

All three Arcturans suddenly explode.

Turn to PAGE 51.

64

You and your friends agree to climb into the egg holes. There's barely room for one of you in each hole.

The larva oozes closer. You hesitate only a moment. Then you place your hands on the edge of a hole and pull yourself up.

The giant eggs feel wet and squishy — and they pulse, like a beating heart. They're covered with a thick, clear goop that has a sickly sweet odor. As you cozy up to the eggs, you feel as if you're drowning in honey.

The crawling larva inches past your hiding place. Its gray flank bulges into the hole.

You hold your breath. You know it's blind — but can it sense you somehow? Are you safe?

Then something happens that makes you stop worrying about the monster in the tunnel.

Go on to PAGE 73.

You follow the Vegan to a big room filled with other four-armed aliens playing flashing arcade games. A big, new-looking game booth stands in the center of the room.

"This is where we fight the Arcturans," the alien tells you. "The new war game has three levels: Red, Yellow, and Blue. You may start with either Red or Yellow. You must win both of them to earn the chance to play the Blue level."

"What happens if we win the Blue level?" you ask.

"The Arcturans will be defeated," the Vegan replies. "We will be powerful, then — and you will return home."

"What if we lose?" Katy asks.

"You mustn't lose!" the Vegan cries. "The game is virtual, but because your brain is connected directly to it, your fate will be quite real."

You gulp. You've never played for such high stakes!

You and your friends sit at the console. The Vegan slips electrodes into your ears. "When you win one level, you'll return here to begin the next," it tells you. "Good luck!"

You and your friends study the console in front of you. A screen above the Red level shows a red-desert planet. A screen for the Yellow level shows a big yellowish-green planet.

To start on the Red level, turn to PAGE 95.
To start on Yellow, turn to PAGE 7.

"I think the lights were red and green," you declare. "Let's try this door."

Andy shrugs and follows you through the red and green door. You find yourselves in a roomful of machinery. Everything there — boilers, wheels, pistons — is white with frost.

The biggest machine has a huge red switch. A sign over the switch says WARNING: DO NOT TURN OFF OR GAME WILL END.

"This is it!" you shout excitedly. "It's the controls for the game! If we turn it off, we'll be free!"

"Wait!" Andy cautions.

Too late — you've already pulled the switch. *KAROOOOOOOOCHMUNCK!* The machinery grinds to a halt.

"Yeowch!" you yell. Your hand feels as if it's burning up!

You try to pull your hand from the icy switch, but it's stuck. It's frozen in place! And it's turning blue with cold.

"Don't pull!" Andy cries. "You'll rip your skin off. Wait, I see a shovel. I'll use it to break the switch."

There's another possibility. If you took the magnifying glass from the ice cave, you could melt your way free.

Break the switch on PAGE 57.

If you have the magnifying glass, use it to melt the switch on PAGE 136.

You spin around in the snow. A huge brown beast is charging straight toward you. It has long, sharp, yellow tusks.

Hey. It's a walrus!

A big, nasty-looking walrus.

You always thought walruses were harmless. But this one seems to have a serious attitude problem. Even worse, it's at least six feet tall. It probably weighs six hundred pounds. Its ugly mouth could swallow you in one bite.

Your heart begins to pound.

You turn and run. But your feet are heavy in the thick snow. You can barely move them. You lunge forward — and fall. Quickly, you scramble to your feet.

You peer over your shoulder. The walrus is right behind you. It moves quickly on its huge flippers. Before you can take another step, the walrus looms over you. Its hot breath blasts your face.

And then you remember something.

Check your memory on PAGE 126.

You, Jordan, and Katy hurry down the stairs. The air begins to feel humid. You can smell wet dirt and plants.

Way above you, you can hear a faint hissing noise. The lizard is still after you!

At last you reach bottom. You find yourselves in an alien greenhouse. Outside, the strong red sun beats down on the tinted glass. Thousands of bizarre plants grow from pots and tubs. The plants are red, yellow, purple, black — every color but green.

You gaze up at a huge cabbagelike plant with bright orange leaves. A purple palm tree grows in a pot by your side. Thick purple sap oozes out of its leaves.

"Cool!" Katy exclaims.

"Nice garden," you agree. "But the lizard is still after us. We've got to think of a way to fight it."

"I've got an idea," Jordan offers.

Examine his idea on PAGE 85.

"Look at your right hand!" Katy gasps. "It's blue!"

You glance down at your hand. You catch your breath.

It's true! Your hand is still blue — the way it was when it was frozen to the switch. It's horrifying!

You duck into a restaurant. "Wait for me," you tell your friends anxiously. "I'm going to run my hand under hot water."

The instant you touch the restroom faucet, it freezes solid. Instead of a normal metal color, it's now ice-blue.

Instead of water, ice cubes tumble out of the tap.

In a panic, you grab a towel. It turns stiff and cold.

"*AAAAGH!*" you scream, shocked. You drop the towel.

It shatters on the floor!

You reach for another towel with your left hand.

Nothing unusual happens. The towel stays soft.

"Oh, no!" you whisper as you realize the awful truth.

The game has permanently changed your right hand. Everything it touches freezes instantly.

The downside is, your friends complain that you always give them the cold shoulder. But don't worry, there *is* an upside.

You'll never have a problem making iced tea!

THE END

The Ice Hound grips Andy in its big, wet mouth. It carries him over to the pile of rags and drops him. The puppies squeal even louder.

They squeal in hunger.

Now the Ice Hound turns around. It heads straight for you.

In horror, you realize that it's dinnertime for the puppies. And that *you and Andy* are supposed to be their chow!

You thought virtual reality was going to be like watching TV — only you'd be part of the show.

But you never dreamed that you would be the TV dinner!

THE END

"I'll tunnel into the snowbank," you tell yourself.

You scoop fistfuls of snow out of the bank. The problem is, new snow keeps filling your little hole. But you continue digging like a maniac. The hole grows bigger.

Soon, it's a small tunnel. You crawl into it.

You're not so cold now.

But the snow, driven by the blizzard, stings your face.

You keep digging.

The hole gets deeper.

You grow even warmer.

Soon you're sweating. But you're in a rhythm now. You make the hole wider, deeper.

You keep digging until you hear a terrified cry: "Fire! Fire!"

Go to PAGE 108.

72

You and your friends step into a plastic booth. You flop down in one of the bucket seats and put on the gloves, boots, and helmets. The helmet comes down to your chest. You can barely see through the dark plastic visor.

"Who turned out the lights?" Jordan jokes.

"I don't like this," Katy grumbles. "I can't see."

"Don't worry," Madame Zapp tells her. "Once the computer is on, you'll see — plenty."

She plugs wires from the helmets into the console. "Which adventure will you pick?" she asks. Her whispering voice sounds like waves breaking against the shore.

"I pick 'Adrift off Vega,'" Jordan announces.

"Me too," Katy echoes.

You hesitate. The poster for "Abominable Snow Woman" looked more interesting to you. But you aren't sure you want to play it alone. It might be more fun to team up with Katy and Jordan.

To play "Abominable Snow Woman" alone, turn to PAGE 97.

To team up with Jordan and Katy in "Adrift off Vega," turn to PAGE 81.

With a sickening, pulpy sound, the giant eggs around you begin to hatch.

You gasp, horrified, as a dozen gray, eyeless baby insects begin wriggling out of their slimy shells. They're not yet as big as the giant larva in the tunnel. But they have the same hideous, hungry mouths, filled with rows and rows of tiny, sharp teeth.

There's nowhere to run. The giant larva is blocking your way out. There's nowhere to hide.

A dozen mouths open and close, open and close.

These babies are starving. And you know what their first meal will be.

You.

Better close the book now. You don't want to know what happens next. Let's just say you've come to an *egg*-stremely disgusting

END.

Cockroaches pour into the tiny spacecraft. One of them approaches the control panel and examines it with its roach antennas.

Others move closer to you and your friends. They extend their antennas toward you. They seem to want to touch you.

Katy and Jordan back up against the bulkhead, screaming so loudly, you can hardly think. It's going to be up to you to save yourself and your friends.

But what can you do? You glance around frantically.

Your eye falls on a fire extinguisher. Maybe you could use it as a weapon.

On the other hand, the roaches seem curious.

Maybe they're intelligent.

Maybe you can communicate with them and persuade them to help you.

Use the fire extinguisher on PAGE 38.
Try to reason with the roaches on PAGE 131.

"The first challenge is a test of knowledge," the first Arcturan tells you. "It is based on a GOOSE-BUMPS book we found in one of your time capsules."

You can't help smiling. You and your friends have read all the GOOSEBUMPS books. There's no way you'll blow this question!

"This is the challenge," the Arcturan goes on. "In *Trapped in Bat Wing Hall*, the members of the Horror Club go on a scavenger hunt. Which of the following is *not* on the list of items to find?
— one human bone
— three hairs from a werewolf
— a straw from a witch's broom
— two claws from a bat
— a piece from a mummy's bandage?"

Yikes. You bite your lip. That's a tough one!

If you've read Trapped in Bat Wing Hall, *you already know the answer. If not, you'll have to guess.*

If the item not *on the list is a human bone, turn to PAGE 12.*

If the item is two claws from a bat, turn to PAGE 23.

"Guys!" you cry, running to them. "Are you all right?"

Jordan raises his head. "We're fine," he replies calmly. "We were just trying to decide which way to go."

Now you see why your friends are lying on the floor. They're gazing into a big, open trapdoor. Stairs lead down one side of the trapdoor. A red plastic slide leads down the other.

You suddenly remember the map that the Vegan gave you. Quickly, you fish it out of your pocket and study it.

"The stairway leads to something called the 'Garden of Doom,'" you announce. "The slide goes to the Pit of Horrors."

"What a choice," Katy mutters.

You examine the map more closely. In big letters it says WARNING. DO NOT APPROACH THE

The rest of the sentence is missing.

HISSSSSS!

"The lizard!" Katy shrieks. "Which way do we go?"

There's no intelligent way to decide. So take this silly test: Do you have a staircase in your own house? If so, climb down to the Garden of Doom on PAGE 68.

If you don't have a staircase, slide on down to the Pit of Horrors on PAGE 129.

Oops. You threw the spear too hard.

It sails far beyond the beast.

The beast turns and races after the spear. It grabs the shaft in its mouth. Then it races back to you.

It drops the spear at your feet. Tail wagging, it licks you with a moist, cold tongue the size of a windshield.

"It's a dog!" you cry in astonishment.

The white dog wags its tail even harder. Its friendly black eyes sparkle. It reminds you of a puppy you once had — except it's the size of your mom's minivan. Dangling from its collar is a dog tag as big as a car's license plate.

"'Name: Abominable Ice Hound,'" you read aloud. "'If found, please return to Abominable Snow Woman.'"

"It must be the Abominable Snow Woman's pet!" Andy declares.

At the mention of its owner's name, the dog barks once, sharply. Then it takes off, bounding over the snow.

"Come on!" you cry to Andy. "Maybe it will lead us to her!"

A mountain range looms nearby. About halfway up one hill, you spot a dark shape. A cave! you realize as you draw closer.

Maybe the Abominable Snow Woman lives inside!

Enter the cave on PAGE 125.

Beneath the snow is a doorway leading down to an underground building made of ice blocks. A sign over the door says:

HEADQUARTERS OF
THE ABOMINABLE SNOW WOMAN.

"Thanks to me, we found her!" you shout.

Andy just snorts.

You pull open the door and rush through. Inside is a big entrance hall. The floors and walls are made of polished ice.

There are two doorways at the back of the entrance hall. The left-hand door is violet and yellow. The right-hand door is red and green.

Which door leads to the Abominable Snow Woman?

It would help to know her favorite colors.

Remember the poster for this game in the virtual reality arcade? How carefully did you check it out? The poster showed kids fighting a fierce-looking creature. In the sky, lights glowed in two colors. Which colors were they?

If you remember, you'll know which door to take. If you don't — take a guess.

If you think the lights were red and green, turn to PAGE 66.

If you think they were violet and yellow, turn to PAGE 34.

"You will be *my* slave," the blue-eyed Arcturan tells you. "The first thing I want you to do is polish my scalp."

The glass case covering your new master glows blue, then disappears. A soft blue rag appears on the tabletop.

You peer at the Arcturan's scalp. Yuck! It's got *major* dandruff!

"I'm not polishing anyone's scalp," you declare. "Forget it!"

"You have no choice," the Arcturan replies. "My brain waves are much stronger than yours." It stares at you. A blue bolt shoots out from its eyes. Blue energy surrounds you. You feel your mind relaxing.

You're in a great mood suddenly. All you want to do is polish a scalp. In fact, you can't wait to get started. You pick up the rag and begin rubbing.

On the other side of the room, you're vaguely aware of your friends taking care of their Arcturans. But you don't care. The only thing that matters to you now is keeping a clear head.

THE END

"We found an even number of words," you tell the Arcturans.

"I knew it!" the blue-eyed Arcturan cries. "Earthlings can't do the puzzle! Too bad — you almost made it. But not quite."

"You mean we can't go home?" Katy cries. Her voice is shaking.

"My dog misses me," Jordan whines.

"I miss my dog," you say. "I even miss my little brother. Please, please — don't make us stay here!"

The Arcturans stare at you. Then they glance at each other.

"Oh, all right," the blue-eyed Arcturan says. "You would make lousy slaves, anyway. We'll send you home. But we have no spaceships. We'll only be able to transport your minds."

"What do you mean?" Jordan demands.

"I mean — you'll be like us. No bodies. Only heads."

Nothing but a head! You're horrified. You can't even imagine what your parents will say when they see you.

But at last you and your friends decide it's better than nothing. At least — finally — you'll be *head*ing home!

THE END

"I want to play 'Adrift off Vega,'" you tell Madame Zapp.

Madame Zapp shrugs. "It's your choice," she says. "But you may be sorry you didn't take my advice."

Before you can answer, she shuts the door to the booth. Through the helmet visor, you see her throw a switch.

Instantly, you're slammed hard into the seat. Your whole body presses against the cushions. You feel as if you weigh a thousand pounds.

A deafening roar fills your ears. It sounds like a thousand jet engines powering up at once. The booth shakes and rocks.

This must be what it's like to take off in a real rocket, you think. It's so cool!

The noise of the virtual engines grows even louder. The booth shakes even more. There's one last, heavy *BUMP!*

Then — silence.

The walls of the booth vanish.

Whoa! Where *are* you?

Find out on PAGE 35.

Quickly, you throw yourself off the snowmobile.

KABOOOM! The explosion hurls you through the air. You tumble head over heels, then land upside down!

Oh, no! You're stuck headfirst in the snow! You struggle, but the snow is packed so tight, you can't move.

"Help!" you try to yell. It comes out, *"HMMPF!"*

Then you feel something pull on your heels. Slowly, your body is dragged out of the icy cocoon.

With a final yank, your head comes free. Groggily, you gaze around.

"Thanks for pulling me out," you mumble, embarrassed.

"Nice driving," Andy says sarcastically. He points to the snowmobile. It's burning up. Flames leap into the sky.

The intense heat makes the ice beneath it sizzle. "Whoa!" you cry. "It's melting a hole!"

Soon there's a huge hole in the snowfield. You and Andy run over and check it out.

At the bottom, you see something that makes you gasp.

Turn to PAGE 78.

Hold on. Did you really think a snowball would slow down a bird the size of Godzilla? Puh-lease!

The bird scoops you into its pouchy beak. You and Andy find yourselves treading freezing Arctic water — along with several seals and tons of fish. Everything sloshes around as the bird swoops through the air.

"Snowballs. G-g-g-great i-d-d-d-dea," Andy complains through chattering teeth.

Without warning, the bird opens its mouth. Half the contents spill out — including you and Andy. You land with a thud in a giant bowl made of sticks and mud. A nest!

The bird flies off. You stare after it. "Why did it let us go?" you ask.

Andy looks glum. "I think it's saving us for a snack."

You peer over the side. The nest sits atop a steep, snow-covered mountain. Clouds ring the base. You can't see what's down there — not that it matters. It would take you hours to hike down. And if the bird comes back, it will pick you off easily.

But then you spot something in the nest.

Something that just might save your life!

Move on to PAGE 116 to find out what it is.

You blink. Hey! You're back in the virtual reality booth! Andy is in the seat next to you. The game has crashed, sending you both back to reality. *Real* reality.

Your friends are standing outside the booth. You introduce Andy to them. "He — uh — he came in after the game started," you say. The truth would just be too hard to explain.

"How was your adventure?" Katy asks.

"It was cool. But maybe a little too real," you admit.

"Ours was bogus," Jordan says. "As soon as we got started, it came to an end. We went to complain to Madame Zapp. But she's gone. All we found was her veil, lying on the floor." He points.

You stare at the pile of gray fabric. Whoa! It's all that's left of Madame Zapp — alias the Abominable Snow Woman!

"I'm hungry," Jordan announces. "Let's go for ice cream."

You and Andy exchange glances. "Uh . . . you guys go on ahead," you mumble. "We'll pass."

"But ice cream's your favorite," Katy protests.

"Not anymore," you reply. Somehow, the thought of eating ice cream leaves you — well — cold!

THE END

"My grandmother used to study lizards," Jordan explains. "She told me that they can't be in really hot sun for more than a few minutes. They'll fry."

"So all we have to do is lure it outdoors?" you ask.

"Oh, right." Katy's voice is sarcastic. "And then we'll fry too. Remember what happened when you tried to go outside?"

"Oh, yeah." You gaze around the greenhouse. There must be something here you can use to protect yourself from sunburn.

"No problem," you tell your friends. "All we have to do is cover ourselves. We can make sun hats from leaves — or try some of that purple palm goo for a sunblock."

Will either idea work?

The only way to find out is to try one.

Make a sun hat on PAGE 117.
Slather yourself in purple goo on PAGE 9.

You glance up to see what's making the shadow. You wish you hadn't.

Above you, a pelican slowly flaps its wings. But this is no ordinary pelican! The mammoth creature has a wingspan the width of a football field. Its pouched beak could hold your entire house.

"I don't believe it," you gasp, rubbing your eyes.

"Me either," Andy agrees. "Pelicans aren't Arctic birds!"

That wasn't exactly what you meant. . . .

The bird swoops down to the water and scoops half a ton of fish into its huge mouth. Then it spots you. It begins circling.

It looks as if *you're* dessert.

"I wish this game could end!" you wail.

But you know it can't. You know it's not a game. It's real.

The pelican flaps closer. Its huge beak opens wide.

Turn to PAGE 119.

As soon as you complete the maze, a scream fills the room.

A scream of triumph.

"YOU CHEATED!" The Abominable Snow Woman starts to laugh. It's a frightening sound, like ice cracking in a stormy sea.

"You didn't really run the maze!" she chortles. "You guessed where to go. But you guessed wrong. You lose! Now you must become a permanent part of the game!"

"No!" you cry. "No, I —"

Before you can finish the sentence, she waves a handheld scanner over you and Andy. "Get with the program, kids!" she cackles.

ZOOP! You're sucked into the scanner. You groan as your body is scrunched and squashed. Help! What's happening to you?

The sad truth is, you've been reduced to a bunch of pixels. You no longer exist, except as a bit of a computer program. And you'll never leave this horrible game now.

Which makes this

THE END!

A bright light flashes somewhere in your brain. You squeeze your eyes shut. Bells bong in your ears.

Then, suddenly — silence. You feel heavy. Very, very heavy. You're so heavy, you can hardly even breathe.

You force open your eyes. Your eyelids seem to weigh twenty pounds. The air is clogged with musty greenish-yellow mist.

Slowly, slowly, you turn your head.

Beside you, Jordan and Katy slump in the swirling mist. They both seem to have become fatter and shorter.

"Where are we?" Katy asks.

"I don't know, but the gravity here is really strong," Jordan replies. His voice sounds low and hoarse.

You touch the ground. It's spongy and damp. You try to stand up. It takes you a long time against the gravity. Your feet sink deep into the mushy ground.

You peer through the mist.

A big yellow blob drifts slowly — very slowly — toward you.

What is it? Get a better look on PAGE 94.

You let the Ice Hound lead you through the long tunnel. At least it's taking you to the Abominable Snow Woman.

Or is it?

You hear a high, squealing noise in the distance. The squealing gets louder. It sounds almost like —

"Puppies!" Andy cries excitedly.

He's right. At the end of the tunnel lies a big pile of rags. On top of the rags you see three baby Ice Hounds. They have long floppy ears and soft pink noses. Each is as big as a full-grown German shepherd.

"They're cute," you tell the Ice Hound. "But where's the Abominable Snow Woman?"

The Ice Hound wags its tail. It seems friendly again. It runs up to Andy.

Then it clamps its huge jaws around his middle and lifts him up.

Andy screams. "No! Put me down!" he yells.

Find out what the Abominable Ice Hound is doing on PAGE 70.

The spear flies toward your chest. You almost decide to let it hit you. A virtual spear can't kill me, you think.

Or can it? Maybe you shouldn't take chances. Besides, you don't want to lose game points.

At the last second you duck. The spear sticks in the snow.

This means war!

"I'm going to wipe out this computer jerk," you mutter. You pick up the spear. "You're history!" you scream, running at your opponent.

"Don't hurt me!" your foe cries. He throws back his hood.

You're shocked to see that he's a kid your age. You stop short — but you keep the spear aimed at him.

"I'm sorry," the kid says. "I thought you were the Abominable Snow Woman." He looks shaken. "My name is Andy."

You tell him your name. "What are you doing here?" you ask. "I thought I was the only one playing this game."

Andy shakes his head. "This is more than a game," he groans. "Everything that happens in here is *real*! You can get hurt here. You can even get killed."

What? *Find out more on PAGE 62.*

You race toward the iceberg. It's already a yard from the snowfield. You flip the spear onto the berg. Then you jump.

You hit the berg headfirst, skidding on your stomach.

Made it!

Back on the snowfield, Andy is paralyzed with fear.

"Come on!" you urge. You hold your hand out.

Andy glances back. The white creature is only a few yards away.

"Here goes nothing!" Andy shouts. He jumps, barely landing on the berg. You grab his hand and pull him to safety.

The berg begins to move faster. You're afraid you'll be swept off into the freezing water. You and Andy lie flat on the ice, digging into it with your fingernails.

"Where is it taking us?" Andy cries.

"Somewhere warm, I hope — like Iceland!" you reply.

All around, you see nothing but cold white ice.

And then you see something else: a huge shadow gliding across the ice.

Go on to PAGE 86.

"We can't take you home," the alien whimpers. "We used up all our power bringing you here."

Your heart skips a beat. Can it be true?

"No!" Katy cries. "I don't believe it!"

"It's true," the alien says. "We had to do it. You are our only hope. You see, for centuries we Vegans have been at war with the Arcturans. We fight all our battles by computer — with virtual reality games. But the Arcturans have invented a new game. A horrible, dangerous game. We don't dare play it. We might get hurt! So the Arcturans are about to win the war."

"So?" you ask. "What does that have to do with us?"

"You must defeat the Arcturans for us," the Vegan replies. "Earth kids are the best game players in the galaxy."

"In other words, you're too chicken to play? You want us to do it for you? Forget it!" you scoff. "Take us home."

"I tell you, we can't," the Vegan insists. "You have no way to get back unless you play the game. If you win, we can rebuild our power supply and return you to your home. If you lose — you will share our fate."

You realize you don't really have a choice.

Like it or not, follow the Vegan to the game room on PAGE 65.

"Let's fight the polar bear," you say fiercely.

Andy grabs his spear. "It's coming closer!" he screams.

"Get ready to throw!" you respond.

"Wait!" Andy cries. "I'm not so sure it's a bear."

"Well, it's huge!" you shout. "And it's after us!"

"*GRRRROOOOOWWWWWWWWWLLLLL!*" the beast cries.

It's only a few yards away now. "If you won't throw the spear, give it to me," you order. "I'll do it."

"Not until we know what it is," Andy insists.

"What does it matter?" you practically scream. "Whatever it is, it wants to eat us!" You grab for the spear.

Andy pulls it back. You wrestle for a moment. Finally, you yank the spear away from him.

"*GGGRRRRRROOOOWWWWWLLLLLL!*" the white beast roars. It's only a few feet away from you now.

In a panic, you heave the spear at it.

Watch it land on PAGE 77.

"What's that?" Jordan cries, pointing at the blob.

"It looks like a pile of lemon Jell-O," Katy announces.

As the creature comes closer, you decide Katy is right. It does resemble a six-foot-tall pile of Jell-O. If Jell-O could have one large, unblinking eye the size of a dinner plate.

SHHHH, SHHHH. The bloblike thing breathes in and out, in and out.

"I wonder what it wants," you murmur.

Straining with effort, you move closer to the creature.

After all, how dangerous could a shimmering blob of Jell-O be?

Move to PAGE 17.

"We'll play the Red level," you tell the alien.

"Our scientists have made a map of the game area for that level," the Vegan announces. "It's not complete. But maybe it will help." It hands you a small scrap of paper. Then it reaches for a red switch.

"When I turn this on," it explains, "you'll be transported to the Red level. Remember: Because the game is connected to your brain, anything that happens in the game will really happen to you. So be very, very careful!"

A chill of fear runs down your back. But you have no choice. Your only hope of ever returning to Earth is to win these games!

You give a thumbs-up sign to Jordan and Katy.

"Ready?" asks the Vegan.

"Ready!" you all declare.

The Vegan throws the On switch.

Start playing on PAGE 27.

The horizon has turned completely white. The wind is roaring like a jet plane. You're about to be caught in a blizzard!

In seconds, the snow is falling so thickly, you can't even see your feet. You try to push on, but the wind pushes you back.

You run into a snowbank and fall on your face. Your mind tells you it's not real.

But to your body, the snow feels hard and cold and wet.

Your parka catches on a piece of ice. *R-R-RIP!* You glance down. There's a hole in the coat!

Worse, there's a hole in *you*! You can see bright red blood where the ice cut your shoulder. And it *hurts*!

Wait a minute! you think. Blood? Isn't that taking things a little too far? You're supposed to be safe in virtual reality.

Inside your torn parka, you shiver. Your shoulder hurts.

Still, you're not ready to end the game yet. Not when you've barely even started to play.

What now? You've read that Arctic blizzards last for days. Maybe you should tunnel into the snowbank and wait it out.

To dig a tunnel, turn to PAGE 71.
To keep slogging through the cold, wet snow, go to PAGE 135.

97

"I'll play 'Abominable Snow Woman,'" you decide. You've always had a secret wish to be an Arctic explorer.

"Excellent choice!" Madame Zapp throws a switch.

Instantly, your body tingles. Bright lights flash. You begin to feel cold. Soon you're shivering.

The flashing lights vanish. You glance around.

The plastic booth is gone! You're no longer sitting in a bucket seat. Instead, you're standing up — in three feet of snow!

A fierce wind whistles around you. Big, wet snowflakes blow against your skin. You're at the North Pole. There's nothing but ice and snow from horizon to horizon!

Looking down, you see that you're wearing a warm Arctic survival suit.

Awesome! you think. This isn't like those dumb VR games you've seen in movie theater lobbies. It's totally lifelike.

You lean into the wind and begin to explore. It's hard to make your way through the thick snow. You want to check out this world. But you're not sure in what direction to head.

And then you hear a hideous grunting noise behind you.

Turn around on PAGE 67.

"Let's take the magnifying glass," you tell Andy. "What good is a compass? We already know we're in the north."

"Whatever," Andy mutters sulkily.

Shrugging, you slip the lens into your parka pocket. "Now all we have to do is find the Abominable Snow Woman," you observe.

"No kidding, Einstein," Andy sneers.

You ignore that crack and suggest, "Maybe the Ice Hound will take us to her."

But where is the Hound? It has vanished.

Then you hear panting. A moment later, the Ice Hound barks.

The chilly dog is standing in front of an opening in the back of the cave. "ROWWWWF!" the dog barks. Its shaggy tail wags.

"Come on," Andy says. "Let's follow it!"

The dog ducks its head and disappears through the opening.

You peer into the opening. It looks dark and slick.

"Wait!" you cry. "Shouldn't we —"

But Andy has already stepped through. Gulping, you follow him.

Step through to PAGE 26.

You start to follow the footprints in the snow. But they lead far into the distance. They could go on for miles.

"Maybe if we wait here, the game will end," you suggest. "Maybe we don't have to find the Abominable Snow Woman."

Andy shakes his head. "I've tried to find other ways out," he replies. "Nothing worked. I'm telling you, we're dead meat — unless we defeat the Abominable Snow Woman."

You sigh. What if Andy is wrong? What if he's lying?

Hey. What if *he*'s the Abominable Snow Woman?

Your heart skips a beat. Then you examine his face. Nah, you decide. He's just a kid who wants to go home. Like you.

You and Andy set off again. It's hard to walk in the deep snow. And who knows how far you might have to go?

"Look! Up ahead!" Andy shouts suddenly.

You squint into the distance. Something bright red gleams against the snow. What could it be?

Hurry to PAGE 123 to find out.

100

You rush to the other end of the iceberg. You grab the spear and hurl it at the humongous pelican.

Amazingly, it flies right into the creature's eye!

"I did it!" you cry triumphantly.

With a dying scream, the gigantic pelican drops out of the sky.

Oh, no! It's plunging down right on top of you! You're about to be squashed by a ten-ton bird!

Smooth move, birdbrain. Now you'll never get out of this Arctic adventure. Instead, you're about to become hamburger — or make that ice-burger!

THE END

"Run!" you shout.

You and your friends race down the tunnel. You're much faster than the larva. Escaping should be no problem.

Except for one thing. After a few hundred yards the tunnel bends — and leads almost straight up. There's no way you could climb it. It's too steep.

The alien larva continues to crawl toward you. It looks as if this is the end. . . .

Or is it? The larva doesn't seem to be slowing down. Is it going to climb the steep slope?

You glance at Katy and Jordan. "What if we jump on its back and hitch a ride?" you whisper.

Try it on PAGE 13.

102

Is there some kind of trick? you wonder. This is the easiest math question you've ever seen!

"The missing number is five," you tell the Arcturans.

The three Arcturans glare at you in stony silence.

"I guess that means we got it right," Katy says with a grin.

"Yes!" Jordan whoops, pumping his fist in the air.

You're feeling pretty good now. "Okay, let's stop messing around," you demand. "Bring on the last challenge!"

"You asked for it," the brown-eyed Arcturan says. It blinks twice, and a grid of letters appears, hanging in the middle of the air. "Here it is. But it's hard. Don't say we didn't warn you!"

Take the final challenge on PAGE 120.

There's no time to think. You jab at the emergency button.

CLICK! The hatch pops open.

WHOOSH! Air begins to rush from the cabin.

A computer voice blares from the console. "Emergency hatch release activated. Ten seconds to total vacuum."

"All the air is escaping!" Jordan yells in terror.

"Shut the door!" Katy cries.

Quickly, you press the button again. Nothing happens.

The air whooshes out the open hatch. It tugs at your clothes, your hair, your skin. You hold on to the instrument panel to keep from being sucked into space. You feel like you're caught in a tornado.

Soon, you realize, all the oxygen will be gone.

And you'll go with it.

Face it. This time you made a bad choice. And, unfortunately, this exciting adventure has come to a breathtaking

END.

"Amazing!" the Vegan says. "You won both the Yellow level and the Red level. No one has ever done that before."

"What about the Blue level?" you ask. "Has anyone ever won that?"

The Vegan shakes both its heads sadly. "Alas, no Vegan has even tried it. You will be the first. All I know about it is that it is a battle of wits between you and the Arcturans."

"You mean all we have to do is outsmart a bunch of aliens?" Jordan asks. He laughs. "Piece of cake!"

The Vegan looks annoyed. "I think you'll find it quite a challenge," it snaps. "The Arcturans are the most intelligent race in the galaxy. No one has ever outwitted them."

Jordan gulps.

"The final level takes place in reality. Step through the gateway to Arcturus," the Vegan orders.

It leads you to a large doorway that throbs with blue energy. Crackling sparks fly from the doorframe. The electricity is so strong, your hair stands on end.

Step through to PAGE 44.

It doesn't take long to figure out the lifeboat's controls. Black buttons fire the engines. You steer with a joystick.

"Cool," Jordan says. "This thing is easy to drive."

"Yeah, right," Katy mutters. "But where can we drive it to? We have no idea where we are."

"Or where Earth is from here," you add. How will you ever get home?

You gaze out the porthole. A pinpoint of light in the distance grows bigger. Soon you can see that it's another spacecraft, shaped like an "X."

"It's completely different from the other alien ship," you point out. "Maybe the people in this ship can tell us how to get back to Earth."

"It's worth a try," Katy agrees. "What do we have to lose?"

A button on the control panel is marked HAILING FREQUENCY. You press the button.

The X-shaped spacecraft instantly veers toward you. It pulls up alongside the lifeboat. You feel a jolt as the big ship locks onto the lifeboat.

WHOOOOSH! Air cycles in the hatch.

A moment later the hatch pops open.

See who's there on PAGE 14.

106

Yes! You won the arm-wrestling contest! You dance around in the snow, flexing your biceps. "I rule!" you shout.

After a while, you calm down. "I'll find the Abominable Snow Woman," you promise Andy. "I'll rescue both of us."

Andy frowns. "Good luck," he mutters. But he doesn't sound like he really means it.

You settle yourself in the seat and turn the ignition key.

VRRRROOOOOOOM! The snowmobile starts up. You grab the handlebars and hang on as the vehicle zooms off.

The wind rushes against your face. Layers of white speed past you. This is the cool VR experience you'd hoped for!

You follow the Abominable Snow Woman's footsteps toward a steep hill. As you get closer, you realize that the hill is the front edge of a glacier. It's a steep wall made entirely of ice.

The footprints lead straight up the wall!

No way can the snowmobile climb a glacier. You slam your foot on the brake.

Uh-oh.

Go to PAGE 10.

"It's almost time for dinner, son," the woman says. "Wash up and come on downstairs."

Son?

As soon as she leaves the room, you run to the dresser. You stare into the mirror above it.

Andy's face stares back at you.

"No!" you cry, panicked.

Andy's mouth forms the word "no."

You can't believe it! But it's true. The Abominable Snow Woman's homing device has put your brain into Andy's body. It's sent you to his home.

You have a horrible feeling that Andy's brain is now in *your* body, in *your* home.

Somehow, you have to find him.

Somehow, you have to find a way to switch back!

But later, as you eat dinner, you realize something very important.

Andy's mom is a better cook than your mom.

Yum! There's no hurry, is there?

THE END

108

"Fire!" the voice shrieks.

You glance around. You're no longer in the snowbank.

But where are you? Thick black smoke fills the air. The smell of burning rubber and plastic chokes you. Your skin feels hot enough to melt. You touch your face and feel the helmet.

You're back in the virtual reality booth — and it's on fire!

Katy and Jordan have already scrambled out of the booth. Ripping off the helmet and gloves, you jump back . . . right into the hands of Madame Zapp.

"You shorted out my control panel!" she shrieks.

Whoops!

It seems you dug your way right through the control panel. You wrecked the virtual reality booth!

You slink out of the arcade. A few days later, Madame Zapp mails you a bill for the damage.

Too bad. Until you pay up, it looks as if your career as an Arctic explorer is on ice!

THE END

The lifeboat bobs around so much, you feel dizzy and sick.

"Make it stop!" you beg.

Katy lurches toward the controls. She grabs hold of the pilot's seat and pulls herself up to the control panel.

The small ship hurtles through space. "I can't stop it!" Katy shouts, working the joystick frantically. She punches buttons. But the small craft only moves faster and faster.

Through the porthole, you spy the alien ship you came from. It swiftly grows larger. You're speeding straight toward it!

"No!" Jordan screams. "We're going to crash!"

You gaze out the porthole in terror. In another moment you'll smash against the alien ship.

Desperately, you crawl over to the control panel. From the floor, you spot a button you hadn't noticed before. It's on the underside of the control panel.

A tiny label says: FOR EMERGENCIES ONLY.

This is certainly an emergency. But you have no idea what the button does. Should you take a chance?

Press the button on PAGE 103.
Brace yourself for a crash on PAGE 30.

As Jordan and Katy dash down the hall, you grab the energy weapon. Its stubby barrel is covered with glowing knobs and dials. You have no idea what any of them do.

Maybe you can fake it. You aim the weapon at the lizard, then back up slowly, ready to follow your friends.

The lizard gazes at you. Its eyes widen. Is it afraid?

Then it makes a strange barking noise: *"HNH! HNH! HNH!"*

Hey! The lizard is . . . laughing!

Claws outstretched, it starts toward you.

You twist one of the glowing dials on your weapon.

Nothing happens.

You try another, and another. Still nothing.

You press a knob on the bottom.

PING! PLINK! KERBLINKITY! The weapon breaks into pieces!

In desperation, you throw the pieces at the lizard. It slips on a ball bearing and falls flat on its face. You take off after Katy and Jordan as fast as you can. You hurtle around a corner.

And then you skid to a stop. Your heart pounds.

Katy and Jordan lie motionless at the far end of the hall.

What's wrong with them? Turn to PAGE 76.

The purple arm pulls even harder.

The blob suddenly lets go. You bounce up as if you've been shot from a rubber band. The hand hauls you into the saucer.

VROOOOOM! The saucer takes off for space.

"Thanks!" you exclaim, drawing a deep breath. For the first time, you get a good look at your rescuer. The creature looks human — except for its purple fur and three-foot-long arms.

"What — I mean, *who* are you?" you ask, trying not to sound impolite.

"I am from Aldebaran," the purple being replies.

"Are you part of the game between the Vegans and the Arcturans?"

"We have nothing to do with that," the Aldebaranian answers.

"Cool!" you exclaim. Just what you wanted to hear. "Um — could you return me to Earth, by any chance?"

"No problem," the purple being says. "I'm heading that way now. It will take a while to get there, though."

"That's okay," you reply. You don't have to be home until dinnertime.

"Good." The creature smiles. "Make yourself comfortable. You'll be home in only three thousand of your years!"

THE END

112

The brown-eyed Arcturan gazes at you as if you were an insect. "Are you Martians ready for the game?" it asks.

"Martians?" you blurt out. "There's no such thing as Martians. We're from Earth!"

The brown-eyed Arcturan looks shocked. "No such thing?"

"Mars, Earth, it's all the same to us," the green-eyed Arcturan says quickly. "The main thing is that you are inferior."

"I can't believe how conceited they are!" Katy whispers.

"Maybe the final game won't be so hard after all," you whisper back. "If these guys don't know there's no intelligent life on Mars, they can't be as smart as the Vegans told us."

"We heard that!" the blue-eyed Arcturan snaps. "Forget it. You won't beat us. The game was designed by our wisest heads. They searched the galaxy for the three most difficult puzzles."

"We can handle them," you declare boldly.

"Unlikely." The green-eyed head yawns. "But if by some miracle you do win, we will end our war with the Vegans and allow you to return to Earth."

"What if we lose?" Katy asks.

"If you answer even one question incorrectly, you and the Vegans will become our slaves forever!" the third head cries.

"Give us the first challenge," you say bravely.

Take it on PAGE 75.

You and Katy slowly rush over to help Jordan. You grab his hands and pull as hard as you can.

The blob won't let go. It moves up Jordan's legs. It begins to cover his body with yellow slime.

Jordan struggles in slow motion. But the blob oozes all over him. Soon it covers everything but his hands and head.

Jordan suddenly stops screaming. His eyes open wide. A creepy smile spreads across his face.

That smile gives you chills.

"Stop fighting it," Jordan commands in a strange, bubbly voice. "Just hold still. It will be all over in a moment. Then you'll be one of us too."

Oh, no! Jordan is one of *them*! He's turned into a blob!

Before your horrified eyes, Jordan's teeth fall out. His hair turns to yellow liquid and drizzles off his scalp. His eyes melt into yellow puddles. His head dissolves.

You suddenly feel something slimy on your hand. The one that was holding on to Jordan. You glance down.

Yikes! A yellow, hand-shaped blob is creeping up your arm!

Quick! Turn to PAGE 37.

114

"What?" you yell. "After all we did for you?"

"Please. Calm down. We'll be happy to take you home," the Vegan assures you. "But first, all my people want to meet you. They want to thank you for saving them from the Arcturans."

"Oh. Well — all right," you grumble. "But make it quick."

The Vegan takes you to a big room decorated with red, yellow, and blue streamers. You, Jordan, and Katy stand on a table, waving and smiling as the room fills with Vegans.

You're still a little creeped out by the Vegans' lidless eyes and ropy arms. But you're glad you were able to help them. They seem so happy.

"Just call me Intergalactic Warrior!" Jordan boasts.

Finally the party winds down.

"Now," your Vegan friend says at last, "it's time to go home."

"All right!" you all cheer.

Zoom home on PAGE 53.

"What's the matter, Katy?" you cry. You and Jordan quickly pull off your own helmets.

Then you understand why Katy is screaming.

Even without the helmet on, you're still in the gray metal room. The alien is still there too.

"What's going on?" Jordan cries. "Why are we still here?"

"Don't panic!" you call. "It must be a glitch in the game."

"It's not a game," the alien says in a hollow, mechanical voice. You notice a metal speaker attached to its neck.

"What do you mean, it's not a game?" you demand. "Of course it's a game! We're in a virtual reality arcade."

"Wrong," the alien announces. "This is real. We kidnapped you from the arcade."

Your head spins. This must be part of the adventure, you think. It's got to be!

"No way," you tell the alien. "This is all part of a computer program."

"Would you like another demonstration of my reality?" the alien asks. Before you can answer, it snakes a long, slimy arm around your neck — and starts to squeeze.

Help! You can't breathe!

Quick! Turn to PAGE 121.

116

The nest is piled with giant bits of broken eggshell. Obviously, the pelican's babies must have hatched recently.

"We're history," Andy moans.

You study the broken eggshells. "Maybe not."

You drag two pieces of eggshell to Andy. The curved shells are two inches thick and three feet wide. "What do these remind you of?" you ask.

"An omelette?" Andy guesses.

"No, dummy. Sleds! We can use these to slide downhill."

Andy rolls his eyes. "You've got to be joking!"

"Well, I'm not waiting for Big Bird to come back," you snap. "Come on, let's try it!"

Try out your new transport on PAGE 127.

"Let's make sun hats," you decide. You scan all the plants in the nursery carefully, looking for the largest leaves.

HISSSSSS! The lizard scuttles into the greenhouse.

It spots you immediately. It zooms toward you.

"Run!" Katy screams. She grabs a leaf from a nearby pink-and-blue-striped tree. You and Jordan do the same. The leaves are big enough to cover your bodies. They're a weird, sparkling blue. You tear open the greenhouse door and head into the desert.

Unfortunately, the leaves make terrible sun covers. In fact, the blue sparkles in them act like magnifying lenses. They make the heat of the sun even stronger!

By the time you discover your mistake, your skin is already sizzling.

Uh-oh. It looks as if your goose is cooked. Any chance you had of winning this game just went up in smoke. But don't get hot under the collar! Just put this book away and try again when you've cooled down.

THE END

118

"Who cares what the sign says?" you declare. "There's no one here to stop us. I say we take both things!"

You pick up the magnifying glass. Andy grabs the compass.

You head for the exit.

Just then, a beam of sunlight straggles into the cave. The beam reflects off the icy wall and hits the polished metal of the compass. By chance, the light reflects off the compass and into your eyes.

"Hey!" you cry. You throw your hands in front of your eyes to block the dazzling light.

Whoops.

You forgot about the magnifying glass in your hand.

The light from the compass strikes the magnifying glass. The lens focuses the sunlight on a big ice pillar in the center of the cave.

You quickly shove the magnifying glass into your pocket.

But it's too late.

How come? Find out on PAGE 41.

You have nowhere to hide on the iceberg.
You've got to do something quickly! But what?
Jump in the water? No, you'll freeze.
How about throwing snowballs at the big bird?
Or — you suddenly remember the spear.
Maybe you ought to attack the monster bird with Andy's spear.
Make up your mind before you get gobbled!

Throw snowballs on PAGE 20.
Use the spear on PAGE 100.

120

```
E  C  A  P  S
A  E  U  L  B
R  I  N  G  L
T  M  G  O  O
H  R  E  D  B
```

Below is a list of words having to do with this space adventure. A few of those words are hidden in the puzzle above. The words run forwards, backwards, up, and down. Find and circle as many words from the list as you can. When you think you've found all the words that are there, count them.

SPACE	BLOB
EARTH	STAR
ALIEN	RING
BLUE	GOO
RED	SLIDE

If you found an even number of words, turn to PAGE 80.

If you found an odd number of words, turn to PAGE 63.

At last the alien relaxes its grip. You gasp for air.

"Now do you believe I'm real?" the alien asks.

You nod slowly. It must be true. You're really in space. The alien really did kidnap you!

"How — how did you bring us here?" you ask.

"Easy," the alien replies. "We built a transport pod to look like a virtual reality booth."

"But why?" Katy asks. "What do you want with us?"

Just then a panel in the wall chimes softly. A voice says something in a weird, whistling language.

"Excuse me," the alien says after listening to the message. "I must leave for a moment. When I return, you will do as I say."

The alien slimes through the door.

"I want to go home!" Katy wails.

"We can't, dummy," Jordan moans. "We're stuck here."

You force yourself to think logically. "If we can overpower the alien somehow, maybe we can force it to take us home."

"How can we fight all those arms?" Jordan protests. "I say we try to escape through that hatch." He points to the small hatch underneath the window.

To fight the alien, turn to PAGE 48.

To escape through the hatch, go to PAGE 28.

122

A deep, booming voice fills the air. "Who broke my machine?"

You look up and see a huge woman dressed in gray robes. Her skin is ice blue. Her teeth are sharp, pointed icicles. White puffs of frost surround her head like hair.

"It's the Abominable Snow Woman!" Andy gasps.

"Ah, so you know who I am," she snarls. "Perhaps you also know the penalty for destroying my things."

"We didn't mean to," you protest. "We just wanted to get out of the game. We thought the switch would turn it off!"

She begins to laugh. It's not a pretty sound. "You thought this switch controlled the virtual reality game?" she thunders. "You've made a terrible mistake. Worse than you know!"

What is she talking about? Dare to find out on PAGE 132.

You and Andy rush toward the shiny red thing. It looks like a small car. But it has skis instead of wheels.

"It's a snowmobile!" Andy cries.

What luck! The computer program has placed a snowmobile in the middle of the ice field. "We'll definitely find the Abominable Snow Woman with this!" you exclaim.

"There's only one problem," Andy points out. "The seat holds just one person. I'll go."

"But I've driven a snowmobile before. I bet you haven't," you object. "I should go."

Andy won't back down. "I've been here longer," he counters.

You frown. "There's only way to settle this," you declare. "We'll arm-wrestle."

To figure out who wins, place a penny and a nickel in one hand. Squeeze the coins. Then open your hand and let them drop.

If the nickel lands closer to your feet, you win the arm-wrestling contest. Turn to PAGE 106.

If the penny lands closer to your feet, Andy wins. Go to PAGE 36.

124

Madame Zapp is the most hideous creature you can imagine. Her skin is blue and covered with icy warts. Instead of hair, icicles sprout from her head. Her eyes flash blue light.

"I am the Abominable Snow Woman!" she thunders. "And you're mine!"

"You're not real!" you cry. "You're just a computer creature!"

"As long as real people play the game, I exist," she retorts. "And that is why I cannot let you leave!"

Andy looks like he's going to faint.

"You fell into my trap!" she tells you with a hideous laugh. "I set up the virtual reality arcade to lure kids into my game. The more people I trap here, the stronger I become."

Oh, no! She wants to trap even more kids. This is terrible!

Somehow, you have to get out of here. You have to stop Madame Zapp's evil plan!

But how?

Turn to PAGE 130.

As you and Andy step into the cave, you're practically blinded. The bright walls and ceiling are made of sparkling ice.

There's more. One wall of the cave is covered with shelves made of ice. On the shelves are dozens of objects: ice-cube trays, cans of instant snow, a ticket to the Ice Capades, a book of fairy tales opened to "The Snow Queen."

Weird.

You spot a sign hanging over one of the shelves: SURVIVAL GEAR. TAKE ONE. SIGNED, THE ABOMINABLE SNOW WOMAN.

Two items lie on the shelf: a gold-rimmed magnifying glass and a silver compass.

"Let's take the magnifying glass," you suggest. "It could help us see small things. That might come in handy."

"But with the compass, we might be able to figure out where we are," Andy points out.

"Come to think of it," you say, "maybe we should take both."

If you take the compass, turn to PAGE 137.

If you take the magnifying glass, turn to PAGE 98.

If you take both things, turn to PAGE 118.

126

You gaze up at the walrus. It gazes down at you.

You grin. Because you just remembered that you're in a virtual reality game.

"Forget it, walrus!" you yell. "You look real. You sound real. You *smell* real. But you're not. No way you can hurt me!"

You break off two long icicles from a nearby ice floe and jam them in your mouth so they dangle down like fangs. Then you roll in the snow until you're covered in white. You jump up in the walrus's face.

The walrus thinks you're some kind of weird polar bear — its natural enemy. With a frightened honk, it backs away.

You growl deep in your throat. The walrus flops away as fast as its flippers can take it.

Yes! Virtual reality rules, you think. It *seems* dangerous — but you can't get hurt. You start chuckling.

A sudden low sound makes you look up. It's like a humming. No, you decide. More like a howling. Then, along the horizon, you catch a glimpse of what's causing the howling.

Your chuckling stops. And your jaw drops.

Find out what caused you to stop chuckling on PAGE 96.

You and Andy take a running start, jump into your shells, and slide down the mountain. It works perfectly.

"Wheee!" you shout. This is fun!

At the foot of the mountain, you tumble from the egg sleds. "Let's get out of here," you urge.

"Uh — we have a problem," Andy says, pointing.

You follow his finger with your eyes. "What?" you ask, mystified. "All I see is the ocean."

"Right," Andy moans. "We're on an island. Trapped!"

You and Andy hurry along the shoreline. Oh, no! Andy is right — the mountain is surrounded by water.

Then you stumble on a small, round structure by the frozen shore. "It's an igloo!" you cry.

You stoop down and enter the igloo. It's empty, except for a piece of paper. You pick up the paper and read:

EMERGENCY SURVIVAL IGLOO
THIS IGLOO IS FOR LOST GAMERS. IT IS
CHECKED ONCE A YEAR. SURVIVAL RATIONS
IN BACK.
SIGNED, THE ABOMINABLE SNOW WOMAN

"Great!" you exclaim. "We've been looking for her!"

"Let's check out the survival rations," Andy suggests.

See what's in there on PAGE 58.

128

"We — uh — we think the missing number is six," you tell the Arcturans.

"Wrong!" exclaims the brown-eyed head. "Hah. I knew you couldn't do it. You have lost your freedom — forever. From now on, each of you will become the personal slave for one of us."

Oh, no! This is terrible!

Still, maybe it's not the worst thing in the universe, you think. After all, what kind of chores could a head with no body possibly need done?

"You'll work for me," the green-eyed Arcturan tells Katy. "From now on, you will do everything I command."

"And you will be my slave," the brown-eyed head tells Jordan.

The blue-eyed Arcturan turns its gaze to you. It smiles.

You can practically hear the thud as your heart sinks all the way down to your toes.

Go on to PAGE 79.

"Make up your mind!" Jordan urges.

"We'll slide," you decide — just as the lizard bursts around the corner and tears down the hall.

Hissing, it leaps at you. Its claws catch on your shirt. The fabric rips as you jump onto the slide. But you're safe!

You and your friends zoom down the slick surface. You glance down. A huge, cone-shaped heap of sand waits at the bottom. It looks like a giant anthill. It even has a hole at the top. Only this hole is big enough to swallow a car.

Faster you slide — and faster. There's no way to stop.

You're heading straight for the hole in the anthill.

And now you see *things* crawling in and out of the hole. Ugly, antlike things with red eyes and jagged-edged pincers.

Well, now you know why it's called the Pit of Horrors.

Dive in on PAGE 133.

130

"Come on!" Andy cries. "Let's find the control center. That's how we'll end the game."

"Hah!" the Snow Woman snarls. "The control center is at the northernmost part of the North Pole. The only way to reach it is through my Ice Maze. But you'll never get there. The maze is so confusing, no one has ever succeeded."

You gulp. "No one?"

"No one!" she repeats. "Especially not two puny kids!"

You square your shoulders. "We have no choice," you declare. "We have to try."

The Abominable Snow Woman laughs. "Go right ahead. But don't say I didn't warn you!"

In a whirl of snowflakes, she vanishes.

WHSSSSSHHHHH! The back of the room slides open to reveal a long hallway. Its walls, floor, and ceiling are all bright white. Frigid air seeps out, numbing your cheeks.

Brrrr!

It's the beginning of the Ice Maze.

Did you bring the compass from the cave? If so, turn to PAGE 134.

If not, enter the maze on PAGE 47.

I'll try to communicate with the roaches, you think.

"We need help," you say. Your voice is shaking, but you try to look friendly.

To your surprise, one of the roaches speaks.

"Why should we help you?" it asks. Its voice is high and squeaky. "This is our territory."

"You speak English!" Jordan gasps. "How — how — ?"

"We monitor your television broadcasts," the bug replies. "Especially the cooking shows. Very interesting!"

Whoa. You're having a conversation with a bug. Yuck!

Still, you've got to try. "Uh — we're stranded here," you tell the roach. "Can you tell us how to get back to Earth?"

The spokesman — make that spokes*roach* — moves closer to you. Two of its hairy claws suddenly shoot out and grab you.

"Ow!" you yell. The claws have sharp edges, like a saw.

Two other roaches seize Katy and Jordan. All three of you scream and struggle. But the roaches are strong. They carry you into their ship and lock you in the brig.

A few days later, the X-shaped ship arrives at the roaches' home world.

Check it out on PAGE 59.

"The virtual reality game is not controlled from here," the Abominable Snow Woman sneers. "This machine makes and throws snowballs for my ice-tennis game." She bends down until her face is close to yours. "AND YOU BROKE IT!"

"We're sorry!" you squeak.

"I'm sure it can be fixed," Andy adds with an eager smile.

"The repairman won't be back for another century," the Snow Woman grumbles. "Until then, you two will make my snowballs."

She hoists both of you under her arms and carries you down a long corridor to a tennis court. There she drops you into a pile of snow. "Get busy!" she snarls.

Quickly, you pack a snowball and toss it to her. She swings a tennis racket at it.

THWACK! The snowball speeds back and smashes in your face.

"More snowballs!" she shouts. "Faster!"

You toss another snowball, spitting snow and ice out of your mouth. "I can't believe we have a hundred years of this!" you groan. "We're going to spend the rest of our lives getting whacked in the face by snowballs!"

"Look on the bright side," Andy says. "The Abominable Snow Woman's favorite sport might have been ice *bowling*!"

THE END

You scream as you shoot into the Pit of Horrors.

WHAP! You slam into a wall of soft sand. It gets in your hair and your mouth. Then you're rolling down a steep, sandy slope.

Katy's sneakered foot whacks you in the head. Off to your left, you hear Jordan yelling.

When you finally hit bottom, you sit up, groaning. The light is dim. But you can see that you're in an underground tunnel.

Holes dot the sides of the tunnel. Inside the holes are dozens of round, glistening packages the size of beach balls.

"Where are we?" Katy asks.

"What are those things?" Jordan demands. He reaches out and pokes one. The round thing trembles at his touch.

"Gross!" Jordan exclaims. "It's all squishy!"

You gaze around at the tunnels and the round packages. It all reminds you of something you've seen somewhere.

The tunnel shakes.

"Someone's coming!" Katy cries.

And now you remember where you've seen this before.

Turn to PAGE 40.

134

Holding the compass in front of you, you step into the maze.

It twists and branches. The compass says you are traveling north. But hours later, you still haven't found the center.

Andy is panicking. "We'll never get out!" he moans.

You slog onward. Then you notice something. At every fork, the walls of one path are brighter than the walls of the other.

You peer at the darker walls. Bits of black rock are embedded in the ice. You hold the compass up to one of the black flecks. The needle swings until it points at the bit of rock.

Hey! The black rocks are magnetic. They're throwing off the compass! No wonder no one has ever completed the maze!

Retracing your path, you take only the branches with brighter walls. Before long, you reach a big white room.

At the far end, the Abominable Snow Woman stands in front of a large control panel. She snarls with rage when she sees you.

Andy points. "That must be the control center. Come on, let's turn off the game and get out of here!"

The Snow Woman holds up a huge hand. "Not so fast! First, you must navigate one last maze. Solve it, and I'll let you go. Fail — and you'll become part of my game forever!"

She waves her hand. A maze of ice springs up, filling the room between you and her.

Try to solve the maze on PAGE 52.

I'll keep going, you decide. After all, you can always take off your helmet and end the game if it gets too tough.

You pick yourself up from the snowbank and slog through high drifts. Hail whipped by the gale stings your face.

No Nintendo or Sega game ever hurt like this!

Then you glimpse movement in the distance.

Squinting, you see something coming toward you.

As it gets closer, you realize that it's a human! A human dressed all in fur, with a big fur hood.

Maybe he can give you some tips on how to beat this weird game! Excited, you run toward the stranger. You're a dozen yards away when he raises a hand.

The hand is holding a spear!

As you skid to a halt, the stranger hurls the spear at you.

Quick! Go on to PAGE 90.

136

With your free hand, you pull the magnifying glass out of your pocket. Sunlight streams in through a small window behind you. You hold up the glass and focus the beam of light on the switch.

Slowly, a tiny plume of steam rises from the switch.

"It's working!" Andy declares.

You soon feel your hand growing warmer. The switch softens. With a hiss, it dissolves in a puddle of red plastic.

You pull your hand free. It's still sort of blue. But you figure it will turn back to normal as soon as you warm up.

The machine makes a popping noise. Sparks shoot through the hole where the switch was. Blue streamers of electricity jump across the room.

"Everything is shorting out!" Andy cries. "Let's go!"

You and Andy rush through the sparks to the door. The electricity makes Andy's hair stand straight up. If you weren't so scared, you'd giggle at the way he looks.

You throw yourselves against the door. An arc of electricity jumps over you and you squeeze your eyes shut. You feel the door slide open behind you. You tumble through.

Open your eyes on PAGE 56.

"We'll take the compass," you tell Andy. "You're right — it could help us figure out where we are." You tuck it in your parka.

"Come on," you urge. "Let's find that Abominable Snow Woman."

But at that moment, you hear a distant rumbling sound.

Spooked, the Ice Hound runs deeper into the cave.

The cave begins to shake. Ice chunks fall from the ceiling.

"It's an earthquake!" Andy shouts.

"Quick!" you reply. "We've got to get out of here!"

You rush to the cave entrance. Outside, a wall of snow and ice is falling from the top of the hill. It's almost covered up the entrance.

"We're trapped!" Andy cries. "The avalanche will seal us in the cave!"

"Quick. Jump out the entrance!" you shout.

You pull Andy with you. The avalanche hurls you down the hill. You tumble along like a pair of giant snowballs.

Land on PAGE 50.

About R.L. Stine

R.L. Stine is the most popular author in America. He is the creator of the *Goosebumps, Give Yourself Goosebumps, Fear Street,* and *Ghosts of Fear Street* series, among other popular books. He has written more than 100 scary novels for kids. Bob lives in New York City with his wife, Jane, teenage son, Matt, and dog, Nadine.

IT'S NOT
UNDER YOUR BED.

Coming December 1997